The CAVES *of* QUMRAN

THE QUEST FOR THE QUEEN

Also by Diamond Wilson

DIAMOND WILSON

The CAVES *of* QUMRAN

THE QUEST FOR THE QUEEN

LonnaDee Press

First LonnaDee Press paperback edition, 2013
Printed in the United States of America
ISBN: 978-0-9898594-2-4
Visit: www.diamondwilson.com

To Joseph. May the truth always guide you.

CONTENTS

The CAVES *of* QUMRAN

THE QUEST FOR THE QUEEN

ONE

Benjamin Pays Double

Benjamin Flickermann's morning had been perfectly normal. He sat behind his desk in ARTIFACTS where he prided himself on finding the rare and the valuable in art and collectibles.

He sat drinking a cup of very strong coffee and looked up as a young man slipped through the door. He wore a scarf around his neck that hid the edges of his square jaw and he tilted his face down like he didn't want to be noticed. He glanced around briefly and then stared at the floor. In spite of his effort to appear unimportant, Benjamin recognized him instantly. The boy looked young for his age, but he was tall and had the strong build of all the Hassan family.

He carried a simple, silver case under his arm. He approached the counter and stopped short, afraid to come too close.

"How can I help you?" Benjamin asked.

The customer stepped forward without a word and set the cylinder on the counter. He opened the top and pulled out a rolled canvas. His fingers danced over the edges gently and revealed a painting no larger than the face of a fireplace.

"What can you give me for this?" he asked. His voice was almost a whisper.

Benjamin looked at him sadly. The painting was worthless. Benjamin sighed. He knew he shouldn't buy it. He was on the verge of saying "no," but something wouldn't let him refuse this boy. Maybe it was the pain behind his eyes or the strain in his voice. Maybe it was because Benjamin saw him for what he could have been rather than for what he was.

Benjamin turned and reached into a drawer. He pulled out 150 sheqels, twice as much as he would sell it for. If it even sold.

"This is the best I can do," he said.

The boy took the money and nodded his head slightly.

"Thank you," he said quietly and turned to walk out the door, lowering his head again as he exited onto the street. He looked both ways and sighed with relief. No one had seen him.

Benjamin shook his head. He moved the painting off the counter and set it against the wall out of the way. Maybe he would have a chance to get rid of it before his wife found out how much he paid for it.

Maybe Benjamin would have lived to see his child born if he hadn't bought that painting.

TWO

Left With Nothing

Johann Barker tried not to tap his fingernails on the edge of the table. Kareem's last words echoed in his mind. *She lives! The Queen wears a disguise, but she lives!*

He sat across the table from Kareem's grandson, a shy boy, no more than seventeen years old. He had shiny black hair and proud eyes that were typically focused on the ground in front of him.

Johann had spent weeks trying to convince the boy to meet with him. "There's something I have to tell you about your grandfather," Johann had said. "Something that no one else knows."

At last the boy agreed.

"Your grandfather died carrying a dark secret," Johann told him over breakfast. He bit his lip and closed his eyes, taking a deep breath.

"Whether you know it or not, I believe that he left you with a clue. Some sort of knowledge that's vital to uncovering the truth."

The boy looked at him blankly. "A clue?"

Johann nodded. "Did he ever tell you anything that seemed odd or out of place at the time? Anything about something called The Queen?" Johann asked.

The young man scrunched his eyebrows, trying hard to remember something. Anything.

Minutes were passing while Johann was waiting for the young man to answer. Johann sighed, stretched his neck, and decided to try again. *Patiently,* he coached himself.

"So…" he said, shifting in his chair and leaning slightly forward in anticipation. The boy's eyes flickered up to Johann's face and back down to his cup.

Teenagers, Johann thought. It didn't please him one tiny bit to be at the mercy of a boy with hardly any hair on his face. This secret that had tormented him for a lifetime was inches away from his grasp and precious moments were slipping away. The boy slouched in his chair, absentmindedly drawing figures in his drink with a tiny straw.

"He gave me something before he died," the boy finally offered. "But nothing to do with any Queen."

"How long ago was that?" Johann asked. He raised the cup to his lips and sipped. The coffee burned his tongue. He added a splash of cream and waited.

The younger man peered into his cup as if the answer were there. Finally, he responded uncertainly. "Three months ago, maybe…"

Johann picked up the cup and blew onto his coffee, sizing up Kareem's youngest grandson. Dark circles rimmed the boy's eyes and his hair was badly in need of a cut. He looked like an injured sheep, Johann thought. Innocent, trusting, and even a little *naïf. Yes,* he decided. *Kareem would have trusted this boy.*

The cup rattled as Johann set it on its saucer and the young man's eyes flickered up at him briefly.

"I take it they didn't give you anything else?" His voice was so dry a match would have lit it on fire.

The boy said nothing.

"The estate, I mean."

The young man just shook his head in response as he stretched his hands, peering at his fingernails. He gave a short, exasperated laugh before he looked up, finally holding Johann's gaze.

"Did you really think they would?"

Johann slowly shook his head.

"So, what now?" Johann asked, stirring his coffee.

No answer.

"What are you going to do?" Johann said again, rephrasing the question.

The boy looked at him bravely, a determination in his eyes that was almost cold. "I can take care of myself. I'll make something of nothing."

Johann grunted at the vexing young man as he paused to sip his drink. It was cooler now. The conversation was lasting too long.

"That's not as easy as you think," he said, setting his cup down and arranging a tip for the server on the table. "Take it from me, I've had a whole lifetime of not enough."

He paused, lowering his voice and leaned in extremely close, so close that no one else could possibly hear him. "You help me get The Queen in my hands, and the story will be different for you!"

"What makes you think I can help you?" he asked. "What makes you think The Queen even exists?"

Johann scrutinized the boy. There was something dangerous in his gaze that hadn't been there before.

"I knew your grandfather better than anyone. You're the only one in the family he would have trusted."

The muscles in his jaw bulged as he gritted his teeth. "And I know it exists because I've seen it."

Johann shook his head in defeat and sighed. He set his hands firmly on the table and pushed himself up and back. He was just reaching for his coat when the young man murmured a name.

"Benjamin Flickermann," he said in a dull voice. "I sold him the only inheritance my grandfather gave me. That's the best I can do."

Johann froze momentarily before he turned to look at the boy. He was telling the truth and Johann's eyes glittered with the knowledge. He rapped his knuckles on the table once in a farewell gesture.

"I'll be in touch," he said and hurried out the door.

"Benjamin Flickermann," he repeated to himself as a smile crept on his face and planted itself on his lips. He hadn't smiled in months.

THREE

A Chance at Adventure

Maylee wouldn't have opened the balcony door if she knew just how much trouble she was inviting in. It was almost dark still, with just the first blush of morning seeping through the glass. The Muslim call to prayer beckoned her with its sing-song wail and she gave in. Opening the balcony door, she slipped out of the room quietly enough not to wake her brother.

The sky blazed with colors, but the houses creeping up the hills maintained still shades of gray, as if the artist who colored the morning had yet to sweep his brush over them. Jerusalem.

As the sun blinked through the clouds with the promise of something new, the smell of grapes and soil greeted her. Parting her lips, she lapped her tongue against the roof of her mouth, sampling the flavor the air carried. Dust and sunshine mingled with the earthy scent of early morning, and that smell had a meaning. A meaning she should know, but couldn't place.

She closed the glass door quietly and turned to watch the sun breathe color into the sleeping city. If only it were that easy for her. Closing her eyes and stretching her fingertips, she imagined stealing a ray of light and swallowing it, painting her insides with the golden warmth. She opened her eyes to find that she was still in the shade.

At least she could think out here in the quiet before daybreak. She hated it when her thoughts were crowded, and she hadn't been able to make sense of anything recently. For two minutes, she would let herself feel. She looked at her watch. 5:41. Begin.

She stuck out her lip and grimaced, straining to squeeze tears from her eyes. Nothing. *This is worse than not being able to sleep at night,* she thought.

Sighing with frustration, she sat on the cool cement to watch a family of ants who were already hard at work, despite the early hour.

A baby ant fumbled with a crumb, awkwardly struggling to hoist the meal when a larger ant came to her aid. They scurried down the crack in the concrete and disappeared. Together.

She, on the other hand, was alone. The feeling made her cold from the inside out. The world had six billion people in it, and she hadn't met one person who understood her.

5:43 arrived and her two minutes were up. Maylee swallowed the bile that crept up her tongue, tucking her feelings away to deal with later.

She cast her glance back over the city just as the sun torched the golden Dome of the Rock and suddenly, she remembered.

"Uncle Arnold's suitcase," she said aloud, the first words in the new day. *That's what Jerusalem smells like,* she thought with a smile, congratulating herself. The scent felt normal, and reminded her of home—a place she was sure would never exist for her again.

"Planning a trip?" a voice startled her.

Consumed in her thoughts, she hadn't seen the boy peeking over the stone wall that separated her space from the neighbors' yard. He was becoming more clearly visible as he scaled a grapefruit tree in the orchard next door. He stared at her with a laugh in his intelligent eyes—eyes that burned on his dark skin like hot tar. Her face turned red and she wondered how long he had been watching her. *Idiot, idiot, idiot!* she scolded herself.

"Hey," she greeted him with equal sarcasm. "Early bird?"

He avoided the question and shrugged mysteriously, swinging his legs around to sit facing her on the fence. He was so close, she could have reached out and touched his knees.

"I'm a lot of things," he said.

Ya, a little voice inside said. *Hot for starters.* Maylee backed up a step.

His mouth curved up slightly on one side in a half smile, watching her eyebrows and wondering if she knew how much her expression gave away.

"You can call me Rafi."

"I'm Maylee."

"So you're from America, Maylee."

"No," she said. She gave him a look that asked, *How can you be so disgusting?* "I'm from the bottom of the ocean, clearly."

He stared into her eyes without blinking. *Is this a challenge?* she wondered. He was so stinking comfortable it made her mad.

"Hmm…" he grunted, letting his eyes wash over her. "A catfish with a sense of humor, I like that."

Maylee rolled her eyes at him.

He popped a grape into his mouth and chewed slowly, laughing silently at her. "So, what brings you out to the balcony so early this morning?"

"I was hoping to have some peace and quiet. You can tell how well that's working out for me."

"Well, that's too bad," he said. He brushed his hands on his pants and flipped around to his side of the wall. "I didn't realize you would be so boring."

"Boring?" she shrieked. "You don't even know me!"

He paused and peeked at her through the branches. "Well, I was trying. I was going to invite you on an adventure, but you prefer peace and quiet. Call it what you want," he said shrugging his shoulders like he didn't care.

He climbed farther down his tree and had just disappeared behind the wall when she called out. "What kind of adventure?"

He didn't answer. *Oh, now I've done it,* she thought. *Now I get to sit around the house all day doing nothing instead of hanging out with the finest guy in Jerusalem.* Maylee got up off the ground and was turning to go back inside when Rafi popped his head over the wall again.

"Are you sure you're up for it?"

"Sure, why not?"

He came closer again, straddling the wall as if he hadn't completely made up his mind that she was worthy. He tossed another grape in his mouth and eyed her carefully.

Maylee licked her lips. The grapes looked good. These

weren't like the ones in the grocery store that were shiny from their wax coating. They were warm and supple, dusted with a white film that made them look frosty. Thrusting out her palm and wiggling her fingers, Maylee silently demanded a handful.

Playfully, Rafi dangled them just beyond her reach. "Share!" Maylee called out laughing, reaching over the balcony and grasping his strong wrist. He let her have them. Her eyes sparkled in victory and she taunted him with a smile, as if she had won. But he knew better. He got exactly what he wanted.

"So," Maylee said, pausing to chew on the grapes, "what's the plan?"

"Midnight, we meet right here. Bring some snacks and something to drink."

Maylee looked at him, confused. He swung back around to his side of the wall and was climbing down.

"That's it? That's all you're gonna tell me?"

Just like a man, she thought, spitting out the rest of the grapes on the ground.

"Wear a jacket…" his voice wafted over the wall from far away.

Neither of them knew how completely unprepared they really were, or how dangerous of a journey they were about to start at midnight.

FOUR

Benjamin Is Missing

The phone rang just as Johann was walking out the door of his apartment. He locked the door and grabbed the phone from his pocket. *Better just see who it is,* he thought.

Had it been anyone else, he would have let it go directly to voice mail. But this call was from Tamarah Flickermann. *Guess I'd better take this.*

"Johann Barker," he answered.

Silence on the other end of the line.

"Hello?" he asked.

He heard a sniffle and a sigh before Tamarah spoke.

"Something's happened."

"What do you mean?"

"It's Benjamin. I was going to take him dinner at the shop since you were supposed to meet late tonight. He's gone."

"I'm on my way right now. We aren't meeting until 8:30."

"That's what I'm saying, Johann. He's gone. And ARTI-FACTS is trashed."

Johann was processing the information. Benjamin, gone. ARTIFACTS, trashed.

"A burglary?" he whispered.

"That's what I'm guessing. I called the police, but they haven't arrived yet."

"Tell me you aren't still there, Tamarah." A warning lit his voice.

"I'll see you when you get here," she said before hanging up.

Johann walked faster. His smile was gone now. Dust from the streets that settled in the wrinkles and lines in his face wasn't the only reason he looked so suddenly gray. A sense of foreboding settled in. Anxiety bunched up in his stomach and made him sick, that awful ball in his gut every time he did something horrible on accident.

This is about the Queen, he thought. On one hand, that meant that he was on the right track. On the other, he never meant to get Benjamin involved.

The nervousness caused his stomach to cramp. He had to get to ARTIFACTS, and the pain was threatening to slow him down. *Just a little ways more,* he thought, focusing on his breathing. He was definitely too old for this.

He felt that the urgent knot in his stomach would burst, ripping through his belly button and exploding him into a thousand pieces. That knot was dread and the imminent need to do something he wasn't capable of fixing. And he couldn't fix the fact that Benjamin Flickermann had disappeared. Or the fact that it was his fault.

Just a few more steps, he encouraged himself. He could see the shop now, see a shape that must be Tamarah. He breathed heavily and trudged forward.

He slowed down and tried to control his breathing. He

squared his shoulders and straightened his walk, preparing to meet the sniffling Mrs. Flickermann.

She stood under the street lamp, wiping her tears with a wad of tissue that was peeling from overuse, leaving little white specks on her nose and cheeks. She lifted up a tired hand in greeting and forced a brave smile. The smile made her feel worse and it crumpled in an effort to restrain her sobs.

Johann paused before the door and gave her a firm hug underneath the orderly sign that read ARTIFACTS in eggplant purple letters. Mrs. Flickermann had painted them herself and had made Benjamin take them down a dozen times and re-nail them up so that they hung perfectly over their little family store. The precision of the letters seemed to chide him as he glanced through the window and saw the mess that reigned inside the usually tidy shop.

"Shh," he whispered as he held her against his shoulder. Righteous anger burned inside him. The Flickermanns were good people. Who could have done this? The place was completely ransacked. Even worse, Benjamin was missing. Kidnapped or killed. The thought caused Johann's eyes to narrow as he peered through the glass.

All the lights were on, as if setting the stage for the papers that were strewn everywhere. A mound of valuables cluttered the walkways. The whole store looked like a child had dumped his toy box onto the ground searching for something to play with.

Paintings and photos had been ripped from the walls leaving great pockmarks in their wake. Drawers were left open and shards of ceramic pointed accusingly at the lights.

A messy line of masks lay scrambled on the floor, some of them crying, some screaming as if in horror of what they had witnessed. The most poignant masks were the ones that held no expression; they were mute and no amount of torture or threat would be able to wring the truth from their voiceless necks.

Johann shuddered at his own thoughts. *Torture the masks? Really, Johann?* His depression was worse than he had realized. He decided to focus his attention on the grieving Mrs. Flickermann and gave her an awkward pat on the back. Comforting wasn't exactly his forte.

He released her and entered the little shop which the perpetrator hadn't bothered to lock after their hurried exit. Tamarah Flickermann stood at the border of the night sky and the florescent lights of the store. She watched him from the doorway as he gingerly stepped over the precious items that lay on the floor.

She couldn't go in there, not yet. She imagined her husband, small but solid as he faced the intruder. She knew what he would say. *"If you can explain what you are looking for, I will gladly give it to you. No violence or police interference is necessary."*

And she knew how he would say it—calmly, steadily, his black eyes warm with compassion. How many times had he quoted the famous words, "Forgive them, they know not what they do," when she had been angry and ranting? Good, excellent Benjamin. Her Ben.

"It doesn't look like they took anything valuable…" Johann said slowly, as if he didn't believe himself as he said it. He didn't, really, because it didn't make any sense. The money, the art, the collectibles; everything was still there.

Tamarah said nothing. She couldn't. They had taken everything from her when they took Ben—her love, her life itself. Her knees went weak and she pushed back against the door jamb, sliding slowly to the ground.

She closed her eyes and pressed her face into her bent knees and silently screamed. No words, just liquid rage that poured from her eyes, her nose, and even her mouth. She looked back at Johann, transformed. Her eyes were flat and empty, as if she had cried the life right out of them.

Johann couldn't even look her in the face any more as she sat crumpled in the doorway, wedged between hate and despair. He called her a taxi and tucked her safely in the cab.

"I'll deal with the police," he said. "How about you go to your mom's house?"

She shook her head. "Home. I want to go home."

Johann gave the driver her address and shut the door just as the police were arriving. He wrote his statement and gave it to an officer, keeping the details to a bare minimum.

Benjamin stayed late. Tamarah found the shop and called the police, then him. The only thing that seemed to be missing was Benjamin.

"Well," the officer said, "there is no sign of forced entry. Nothing was stolen. Mr. Flickermann is not here, but nothing at this point warrants a missing-persons investigation. If we have any questions, we'll contact you or Mrs. Flickermann."

Johann just shook his head. Nothing to warrant a missing-persons investigation! He understood the officer's perspective, but he knew differently. Something was dreadfully wrong, and it had to do with the Queen. He thanked the police and locked up ARTIFACTS with the key Tamarah had left with him.

As soon as the police were out of sight, he set off in a trot up the street. His heart pounded in his ears and the air seared his old lungs. One thought kept replaying in his mind. *Someone else knows.*

The only logical answer to all of this was the boy, but something just didn't add up. His gut told him Kareem's grandson was innocent. Regardless, he planned to keep a close eye on the boy, and his vigil started now.

FIVE

Ghosts in the Grove

Rafi whistled into the night twice, signaling that all was clear. Maylee and her brother Smith crept silently from their room into the quiet darkness of the night. The stars seemed to hurry them on with urgent bursts of energy as they stretched across the balcony and onto the wall, letting themselves down by the tree on Rafi's side.

"Everything is ready," he whispered, displaying a canvas bag holding goat cheese, a loaf of fresh bread, and some almonds.

Maylee and Smith held up two large metal bottles filled with water, as well as some M&M's. The sleeping city was as still as a photograph and the trio meandered its silent streets with only the moon as their chaperon.

Maylee finally let out a nervous giggle. "I've never snuck out before!" she said in a half-whisper.

"Ya, our mom would totally kill us if she found out. Which is why…" Smith paused and a devilish grin transformed his angel face. "What happens in Jerusalem, stays in Jerusalem."

Rafi's voice held an edge as his words sliced the night. "This is nothing," he declared a little too loudly in an effort to sound very grown-up.

He paused arrogantly, snatching up a stray stick. Maylee and Smith halted.

"I go lots of places," he continued, dragging the stick along the ground and creating a trail of white dust. "Places that aren't even safe in the daytime—places where they cut your head off before they ask your name."

He made a slicing motion with his hand across his neck. "I took some raisins to sell to old al-Rashad once. His cousin had a machete to my throat before I even had the chance to whistle."

He paused, looking at them sideways and snapped the stick in half dramatically, tossing it to the side before he continued. "But lucky for me, al-Rashad recognized me just in time."

Smith raised a hand to his precious neck, but Maylee was unaffected. She was thinking, actually, that if someone severed your head from your body, at least you had a reason to feel like you were dying.

"I heard that when they cut your head off, you can still be conscious for a few seconds afterwards, even see your own body lying there dying," she shared.

Smith gave her a blank look. "You're so weird."

"I'm serious!" she argued. "It's something like eight seconds."

"Well," Rafi said with a smile, "If you really want to know, all I can say is ladies first!"

Smith snickered and a broad smile painted itself on Rafi's lips.

"Whatever," Maylee said, annoyed. "I hope they don't recognize you so quickly next time."

Up they climbed on the weaving trail, the rocks worn smooth, pounded by sandals and tennis shoes that trod that very path for thousands of years. The friends held a sort of sacred silence as they neared the Garden of Gethsemane, the dark mass of the Mount of Olives looming in front of them.

Smith peered behind them every now and again and Maylee could hear his heavy breathing. He was probably scared, and Maylee could understand why. Nights this quiet were just downright creepy. It wasn't hard to imagine that someone was sneaking up on them from the rear.

Rafi spoke, breaking the silence. His voice was strangely flat in the still night. "It's not very far to the Garden," he said, "but we have to circle around to the back side. The wall has a little hole we can slip through."

Sparse bright patches on the white ground where the moonlight reached the earth lay among the shadows of rocks and trees, creating a sinister chessboard as Maylee picked her way over roots and jagged stones.

A mouse made a wrong move into the light, frightened out of hiding by the sound of their footsteps. It shrieked as an owl swooped down and snatched it up in his sharp talons, disappearing again into the cover of darkness. Checkmate. Maylee shuddered, moving closer to Rafi who was guiding them toward the back of the wall.

The moonlight danced on the layered stones, illuminating the years of history that lay etched on their surface. The old wall remembered the lovers who had engraved their names side by side in the stone, the hands that had traced the bumps mindlessly, and the tears of those who came to remember.

It kept sinister secrets too, its lips sealed with thick mortar. The old wall was too young to remember the smack of Judas' kiss long ago, dripping with betrayal. Tonight, however, it would stand as a silent witness to crimes against another innocent man.

A hole gaped at them as they reached the back of the Garden, reminding Maylee of a weathered, toothless woman she had seen smiling in a museum photo. Smith poked his head through. "Wow!" His voice sounded hollow behind the stone. Maylee gave him a shove, toppling the rest of him through the gap so she and Rafi could follow.

Thick, gnarled trunks squatted into the ground, their branches turned and twisted as if they had frozen in the middle of a dance. Some of them looked almost human with old, wrinkled faces and twiggy mustaches, reaching out with stubby arms and green fingers.

Maylee looked at one tree in particular. It stared back at her and the fissured bark in the tree looked like frown wrinkles. *You would be wicked if you had a soul, wouldn't you?* she thought, running her hands over its rough trunk.

The atmosphere of the garden was heavy with opposites. Prayer and weeping, friendship and betrayal. Life and death. Strangely, the heaviness comforted Maylee. It felt—real. She could feel it on her skin and smell it in the air. She felt at home here in the dark. The quiet thoughts she didn't share with anyone were free to waft around the garden, safe in the confines of the trusty wall that housed everyone's secrets.

"I'm gonna find the place Jesus was praying when he was betrayed," Smith announced.

"Whatever, dork," Maylee said. "What are you going to do? Look for sandal footprints?"

"No," he said, shaking his blond head. "I'm going to close my eyes and pray. I'm going to let the spirit of the Garden lead me. Unlike you, some of us do have the faith of a mustard seed."

"Okay, Smith. Let me know how that works out for you," she said.

Maylee closed her eyes and lost herself in the silence of the Garden. Crickets chirped and a breeze rustled the leaves.

Out of all the instruments man has created, none can compare with the sounds of nature, she thought.

"Dang it!" Smith shouted. "I accidentally peeked. Now, I have to start all over."

So much for peaceful silence, Maylee thought. It was nice while it lasted.

She felt someone or something staring at her. Suddenly she felt very awkward and quickly opened her eyes. Her gaze met Rafi's. *How long has he been staring at me?* she wondered.

She felt uncomfortable and exposed. She wrapped her arms around herself and glared at him. "What?" she asked defensively.

He didn't answer. He just kept staring at her with his smoldering eyes, daring her to read his thoughts. His gaze flickered down to her lips and back up to her eyes again. He barely raised one eyebrow as if in question.

Maylee felt her face flush. She ripped her eyes away from Rafi. It was all she could do not to bury her burning face in her arms.

Smith finally stumbled upon a tree. "I've found it!" he

yelled triumphantly. "This, my fellow friends, is the place where Jesus prayed." He proudly displayed a gnarled trunk.

Maylee rolled her eyes and Rafi suppressed a chuckle. "They don't even know if these are the same trees that were here 2,000 years ago, Smith," Maylee said. She patted him gently on the shoulder and whispered sadly, "I think your faith is a little weak."

"Hey, knock it off," he said, punching her arm.

She laughed and Smith pouted. Rafi waved them toward him.

"Hungry?" he asked temptingly, reaching for his canvas sack.

Smith got there first. He stuck his face above Rafi's pack and peered down his nose at the items inside. "What's that?" he asked, pointing at a white object wrapped in plastic.

"Cheese," Rafi replied.

"That doesn't look like cheese…" Smith said.

Maylee interrupted as she joined them. "That's because it's goat cheese, Smith," she said. "We're in a different country, remember?"

Smith looked warily at the pie-shaped slice and sniffed at it. "Oh, no way! I'm not eating that!"

"Just try it," Rafi encouraged smoothly, licking his lips. He turned and looked boldly at Maylee. "You never know until you try."

For some reason, Maylee blushed. She had a feeling Rafi wasn't just talking about cheese.

Rafi spread several pieces of bread with the creamy substance, topping it with carefully placed almonds. Surprisingly, it was sweet and rich, with the slightest tinge of honey to its flavor. "See?" Rafi said ruffling Smith's hair. "You never know what you might like."

The leaves sang in the trees as a breeze gave them voices, performing their symphony on a stage dazzling with starlight. Maylee silently mused that the moon she saw from her bedroom window in Montana was the same moon that peered down at her through the curtains formed by the branches of the olive trees. She smiled slightly and sighed. Somehow it comforted her to know that no matter what, some things never change.

Rafi was about to wipe a bread crumb from Maylee's mouth, but he clasped her arm instead. A mix of anger and pain flashed in Maylee's eyes as she started to jerk away. He had hurt her and she didn't understand the roughness.

Maylee was about to blurt out something angry to Rafi, but the words caught in her throat as she saw the urgency on his face. He looked scared. Holding his finger to his lips in a silent warning he motioned his head toward the wall.

She heard it too. Something was out there. Straining their ears, the three listened for another sound. Whatever it was, it crunched slowly along the rocks that bedded the path they had followed into the garden.

Their breathing pounded the silence as their adrenaline rose. Still they waited, motionless except for the hairs that rose uncontrollably on their arms. A twig snapped. It was coming closer to the hole. And toward them.

The silence that followed was worse. It must have crossed onto the grassy ground directly outside the wall. The thing could be anywhere.

Maylee scanned the top of the wall, afraid she would

find a pair of glowing eyes watching them, laughing at them before it swooped down and snatched them up. Like the poor little mouse. But this time, they would be in checkmate.

Maylee had a strange urge to give in to the terror, to scream and run recklessly through the garden. Instead, she sat petrified.

A loud scraping sound grated like fingernails on a chalkboard where something dense scratched along the wall, followed by a sharp, low curse. The voice was unmistakably adult. Why would any grown up want to sneak into the Garden of Gethsemane in the middle of the night?

Rafi motioned Maylee and Smith toward the trees. Quickly, almost silently, they both shot up a different trunk, tucking themselves safely away in the branches.

Rafi snatched up their picnic and shoved everything into his canvas pack, was beginning to scale a tree of his own when his knife fell to the ground. The Cheshire cat in the sky smiled down on the blade and lit it up like a flashlight.

Rafi halted as voices approached from the other side of the wall.

"Jack, you come through after me," a man said, panting. This time, something hit the wall with a dull thud directly by the entrance. The voice continued. "We'll have him hoist it to us from the other side."

Rafi acted. He let go of the tree, landing on the ground like a cat and sprinted, snatching up the blade and heading for Maylee's tree. He had climbed just far enough to be out of sight when a large head filled the gaping hole in the wall.

A man peered around the garden with mousy eyes,

slowly moving his fat head and rippling the extra skin in his neck, making him look absurdly like an overgrown iguana. He had a slab of greasy hair that stuck to his sweaty head like fried Spam and he puffed out his cheeks as he strained to recover his breath. Slick with sweat, the fat man slipped through the hole like a wet potato and with surprising speed, sprang to his feet.

Jack's scarecrow face appeared second in the hollow and was immediately followed by his lanky body. He was long and lean like an eel, all one tangled piece with thin arms that got caught awkwardly behind his knees as he tumbled onto the hard ground.

"Shh!" Big Dale hissed at him. "You want someone to hear you?" he said gruffly to Jack who was still trying to pick his crumpled body off the garden floor. Jack gave him a look of gratitude as Big Dale turned and snatched him up off the ground by his collar, shaking him as one shakes the wrinkles out of a creased shirt.

"Aw, don't be so uptight about everythin' Big Dale," the scarecrow said in a bland drawl, "you know dead people can't hear for beans." He paused before laughing at his own comment, a slow chuckle that made the same gluc-gluc-gluc sound spoiled milk makes when you have to pour it all out.

Big Dale was not laughing. He was surveying the garden, kicking at the rocks under Smith's tree with his dark boots. He swore as he kicked the ground, colliding with a huge tree root that lay just below the surface and stubbing what was, based on his general appearance, a very ugly toe.

"Hold up, Jerome," he called over the wall, turning slowly on one foot, crunching the rocks under his thick heel.

He continued in a lower voice, as much to himself as to his partners. "Maybe our ghost would be more comfortable in the graveyard…"

SIX

Let the Dead Bury Their Own Dead

The bulky American said *would* thoughtfully, as if he were talking about a house guest and not a man he had just murdered. Big Dale reached up into the tree where Smith was hiding and plucked a green olive. His hands were massive and hairy, with loose skin that covered them like ill-fitting gloves. He was spinning the olive thoughtfully between his fingers and decided to crush it just as Jerome shoved head and shoulders through the hole.

"I told you the soil wasn't deep enough to bury a man here," he growled. His accent when he spoke English was perfect, Smith noticed. His voice was different from that of most of the Israelis, who sounded like they had dipped their tongue in candle wax when they spoke English.

Big Dale glowered down at him. "I suggest you shut up," he said pointing a thick finger and raising his voice. "There is plenty of space for your dead body in the graveyard too."

Jerome murmured something in Arabic and disappeared back through the hole.

"Move, idiot," Big Dale said to Jack, shoving him toward the hole. "You think fatty Ben here is gonna bury himself?"

Jack made a sluggish effort across the garden to the entrance, rubbing his sore arms and sighing. "Let's take a break, Dale," he suggested. "I'm awful tuckered out."

Jerome appeared again in the break in the wall. "Come on, we don't have all day! I still have to get back and find the Queen before day breaks and someone notices that he…" Jerome paused, gesturing with his head toward the body outside the wall, "is not coming back."

Big Dale paused thoughtfully. "You're right," he said. "Get out of here. Jack and I will take him to the cemetery."

"Wednesday night, same time?" Jerome confirmed. "Meet back here?"

"Yeah," the big American grunted. "Don't try to contact me until then. And don't try anything funny. If you don't make it, it better be 'cause you're already dead."

"I'm not a coward," Jerome sneered, "I'll deliver what I promised." He disappeared and they could hear his quick footsteps hurrying down the Mount away from the Garden.

Dale threw a last glance around the grove, making sure there were no traces they might have left behind. He motioned to Jack and the two disappeared into the blackness on the other side of the wall.

Maylee's teeth shivered as she heard the scraping sound again. Jack and Big Dale grunted as they lifted something heavy. Slowly, their heavy breathing faded away as they climbed higher up the Mount. Rafi quietly slid down his tree and bounded towards the wall with the hole. He scaled another tree that gave him a vantage of the other side of the wall and he peered over. Maylee and Smith quickly joined him.

Big Dale and Jack were struggling with a large piece of wood, balancing something on top of it; undoubtedly that was what had thunked and scraped along the wall. It took the three friends a moment to identify exactly what was on top of the plank the American men were carrying. It was the body of a dead man. They had strapped him hastily to a wooden plank by several belts, and his body flinched and wobbled with their unsteady steps.

He wiggled so much, it almost seemed as if he were dancing on the board. *The dancing dead man,* Maylee thought with a gulp. She tried to channel her thoughts away from the sinister picture, but the dam was already broken and they rushed through her brain like a storm. Maylee shuddered as she imagined the dead man's ghost jogging through the olive grove, pausing to snap his fingers and dance with crooked trees when no one was watching.

"They are headed to the old Jewish cemetery," Rafi whispered, rescuing Maylee from her imagination. "Let's get out of here!" Maylee and Smith didn't have to be told twice. They dropped a few feet onto the ground and the three of them quickly crawled out of the hole and rushed back towards the safety of their neighborhood.

"Try and get some sleep," Rafi instructed as they neared their houses. "I don't think any of us need more trouble for one night."

"We have to do something," Maylee said. "We can't just let Big Dale and Jack get away. They murdered that man!"

Rafi chewed on his lip thoughtfully as he considered her point. "Tomorrow I'm going to market," he said. "I'll figure out a way for you both to come with me." He raised one eyebrow as an idea filtered its way into his thoughts. "Plus," he added mysteriously, "we just might find some answers tomorrow if we ask the right questions in the right places."

Smith and Maylee looked at him with a blank expression. Maylee didn't figure the answer was stamped on some piece of fruit at the market. Rafi waved his hand at them. "Tomorrow, I'll explain."

Half annoyed at not knowing the details and half relieved that they could deal with it tomorrow, Smith and Maylee swung themselves up the little tree in Rafi's orchard and eased themselves over the gap onto their own balcony. Rafi waited until they had successfully opened the door and gave them a little nod. Turning, he entered his own home and curled up on a giant cushion that served as his mattress. He willed his eyes shut, but the things he saw behind his eyelids frightened him more than the darkness. When he finally fell asleep, it was with eyes wide open.

* * *

The friends had left something more than just the darkness behind them as they made their way home. Moments after they had crossed the grass and back onto the rocky path, a bush shook quietly near the edge of the wall.

A tall figure shadowed by the night slipped from his hiding spot, brushing leaves and dirt from his clothing. A spider scrambled down his back and retreated into the darkness of the night.

The moon cast a sliver of rays that danced on his bald head and illuminated the face of Johann Barker. "So," he thought aloud, pausing to crack his thumbs. "Now we all know." He began to make his way carefully down the path, his dejected figure keeping a safe distance as he followed the children's shadows away from the Garden. His head hung low from the guilt that he couldn't leave trapped behind the walls. The gnarled branches pointed at him accusingly, like twelve men on a jury. *Condemned in the death of one Benjamin Flickermann.*

SEVEN

A Family Heirloom

Jerome made good speed back down the Mount and toward the city. He felt terrible. When he had arrived at ARTIFACTS earlier that day with the Americans, Benjamin had bowed slightly to him and smiled. A sign of friendship, and of respect. They were just supposed to ask him questions. Now, he was dead.

Jerome wanted to shove the image of Benjamin's bruised neck from his mind. Big Dale and his filthy hands had clamped down on the honest man's neck in frustration as he tried to get answers from Benjamin. *Answers that he clearly didn't have,* Jerome thought, his anger toward Big Dale burning deep in his chest.

Jerome wiped the sweat from his forehead with the back of his sleeve and tried to swallow the lump that was rising in his throat. The smell of death lingered on his clothing and hair, and adrenaline only heightened his senses. He slowed to a walk and glanced up and down the street. He noticed that someone had been to ARTIFACTS before him. The lights were still on, but someone had bothered to lock the door.

He reached into his pocket and with a heavy heart,

removed the keys he had taken from Benjamin's body. He shuddered as he thought of Benjamin sharing a grave with an unknown brother. Benjamin deserved better than that. Jerome slipped into the store, taking in the chaos that screamed at him.

He felt like he was watching fuzz on a TV screen. The disarray enveloped him, but none of what he saw meant anything to him. As a matter of fact, he had no clue what he was looking for.

He stroked the rough wooden desk where Benjamin normally sat and picked up the picture of Tamarah and Benjamin that had been knocked over. Jerome's heart ached for the young wife Benjamin had left behind, and frustration toward his younger cousin nipped at him. Why had the boy involved Benjamin in this?

Jerome was setting the picture down when suddenly, he saw it out of the corner of his eye. He glanced up to bring the object into focus. It lay on the floor, slightly folded as if it had slipped down after being propped against the wall.

Jerome shook his head in disbelief and a sigh slipped out of his mouth. He instantly thought of his grandfather. "I would never have imagined!" he said to himself, picking up the object carefully. The Queen was indeed well-disguised, but to his eyes, unmistakable. He had seen it so often that he never recognized its importance. He snatched up a protective art case and in it, he carefully deposited the ugly painting that had hung on his grandfather Kareem's office wall for as long as Jerome could remember.

EIGHT

A Call to Ms. Davis

The alarm clock wouldn't stop beeping. Jerome bobbed in and out of reality and dreams as he lay on his back, trying to wake up. He shuddered and with a definitive smack, he turned the alarm off. The screeching reminded him of Benjamin's garbled screams.

Way too short of a night for such a long day, his body complained as he rubbed the back of his neck. He had a headache that didn't plan on going away any time soon. *That I can deal with,* he thought as he opened the drawer on his nightstand and pulled out a small white bottle. Three coated pills spilled into his palm and he threw them down his throat. No water. He was a pro at this.

What he couldn't deal with so easily was the guilt that had shredded his insides. He was convinced that at any moment, he would vomit and it would be filled with blood. He thought about letting himself vomit just to convince himself that he wasn't dying. But, he was afraid that once he started, he wouldn't be able to stop.

He moved from the bedroom into the bathroom, habitually making the bed on his way. He stared long and hard into in the black framed mirror, analyzing his own face. He was pale and his eyes were bloodshot, as if all the blood in his face had pooled in his sunken eyes, drowning them in a sea of red. How long he stood there, he didn't know. Five minutes? Ten?

His conscience was screaming at him. *It's your fault! You should have stopped him!* He splashed cold water on his face, but his conscience didn't seem to mind. *You're just like them...* "No!" he croaked aloud. *Guilty by association...* "I tried to stop him," he whimpered. *Not hard enough...* it taunted. *Your fault, your fault, your fault.*

His moral sense was in a rhythm now. It sneered at him in the mirror as he saw himself for what he really was. A coward. A spineless, over-educated, selfish coward. *Who didn't have time for this discussion with his inner man!* he realized as he glanced at his watch.

One thing was for sure. He didn't want to meet Big Dale in the Garden again on Wednesday night. Jerome was sure the painting he found was indeed the Queen, and hopefully, that meant no one else had to die.

You deserve to, his subconscious whispered.

He stifled the thought. What if he could get the painting to her sooner? The idea grew in his mind and lifted his spirits. Yes! That would be good!

He brushed his teeth quickly and went back into his room. He swept past the bed and picked up the art case that lay on the ground next to him all night. He would just take it with him. After all, she couldn't possibly be mad about getting it early. And, he knew just how to get her there.

He quickly dressed and grabbed a muffin to eat in the car, rushing out of the house. The drive to work wasn't too long, but it would give him time to eat and make the phone call he needed to make.

He started the motor and connected his cell phone to the Bluetooth. As he sped along, he made the call.

"Jenny Pruitt for Francine Davis," a sweet voice responded.

"Good morning, Ms. Pruitt. This is Jerome Hassan from Qumran National Park."

"How can I assist you today, Mr. Hassan?"

"I would like to request the professional opinion of Dr. Davis on a new discovery in Qumran. Given that she is currently in Israel, I was hoping I might be able to contact her."

"Certainly, Mr. Hassan. I am not at liberty to give out her contact information, but I would be happy to take a message and pass your number to her."

"Thank you," he responded quietly. "Err…and it's quite urgent."

"I understand, Mr. Hassan."

He gave her his cell number. He was about to hang up, but decided on one more thing. "Ms. Pruitt?"

"Yes, Mr. Hassan?"

"Could you add one more detail to the message?"

"Of course, sir."

He inhaled sharply. This was a little risky. "Could you please tell Dr. Davis that her research has influenced me greatly? Enough that I decided to name my daughter Hadassah."

Jenny paused on the other end of the line. *Rather an odd statement,* she thought. *But,* she reminded herself, *my job is to take messages, not to think about them.* Something Ms. Davis was constantly telling her.

"Certainly, Mr. Hassan. Congratulations on the birth of your daughter."

"Thank you, Ms. Pruitt. Have a wonderful day," he said as he hung up. Hadassah. The Hebrew name for a young girl who became Queen.

NINE

A Meeting With Old al-Rashad

Maylee and Smith couldn't wait to get out of the house. Not thinking about what they had seen the night before was next to impossible, and having to keep it all inside was even worse. Uncle Arnold's young Arab liaison certainly wasn't helping matters. He was following them at a distance, but Maylee felt that he was breathing down their necks, spying on them with his beady little eyes.

It had been part of the deal. If they wanted to leave the house, Amjad would keep an eye on them. It was dumb, in Maylee's opinion, because he wasn't very much older than Rafi. Amjad's stony face implied that he really didn't like it any more than Maylee did.

"I'm taking you to see old al-Rashad today," Rafi said in a low voice, glancing around to make sure no one was listening to them. "He will buy the grapes, but he will also give us information. He likes to buy and sell secrets as much as anything else."

As they walked, Rafi shifted the basket he carried, heavy with fruit. Great stands laden with produce, grains, and spices lined the streets as they entered the open-air Mahane Yehuda market. Vendors and buyers haggled over prices. A little girl stood cemented to the middle of the street, wailing over some shoes that no one would buy for her.

Rafi nodded to a group of girls who were huddled around a selection of fabrics and they giggled and blushed when he walked past. The bravest one of the group pulled herself out of the crowd and met him, allowing her hand to brush over his powerful bicep. "Hi, Rafi," she said shyly before sauntering back off to her group. A flirtatious smile danced on his lips and suddenly, Maylee hated that girl with her black braid and white teeth. Teeth that white and straight were on the border of being annoyingly perfect.

Somewhat self-consciously she stuck her tongue through the little gap between her front teeth. It wasn't a big gap, and it was slowly but surely disappearing as her bigger teeth in back pushed it forward. Regardless, she still didn't want to open her mouth for a while.

Somewhere between a shop sprinkled with brightly-colored scarves and a store full of wood depictions of religious figures, Rafi turned sharply down a narrow alley. It was dark and shadowy in spite of the bright day, and it took a moment for their eyes to adjust to the transition from the light. They were surrounded by crude stone walls on either side, connected at the top by strings chalk full of drying clothes that stole the sun. Smith tugged at Maylee's shirt and giggled, pointing for her to look up. A pair of underwear hung precariously from the height, threatening to fall any moment on their heads.

Rafi slowed his pace and put a finger to his lips. He whistled a short tune, and instantly, a wooden square flew out from the wall a few feet in front of them. A terribly old man popped his head out and squinted at them from eyes that were already struggling for space amongst the folds of skin that surrounded them. Old al-Rashad.

The man looked like a human raisin. He was so skinny his elbows seemed to be the biggest part of his fragile body. He waved them to the door with a hand crusted with yellow fingernails.

If Maylee had felt bad about her smile before, she certainly didn't now. He opened the door and greeted them with a nearly hollow mouth that had dried spit in the creases. When he breathed, rotting air escaped from the divots in his mouth where his teeth used to be.

His clothes were tattered and the raggedy ends fluttered in a dance with every jerky movement he made as he bounced around them. He sprung up behind Rafi and stood on his toes to look in the basket. He chortled out a greedy laugh that bordered on insane and then paused, as if frozen in time. Resting his hands on Rafi's shoulders, he slunk behind him and slowly approached Smith.

Smith stared at him in horror, imagining that al-Rashad was going to pull a dagger from the shreds of his garment and cut his throat since he didn't recognize him. Instead, the old man slowly raised a shaky hand and gingerly touched Smith's fair hair. Al-Rashad grinned, his cheeks hollowing, and clapped his hands together, bouncing on two feet to the table like a kangaroo. The old man dug his fingers into a squat jar, and pulled out a crumpled bill and several coins. Rafi scooped the sheqels away from him, but left them on the table.

The wizened old man understood Rafi's intention to buy

a secret because he leaned across the knotted table toward Rafi and turned his head, pointing to his ear. Rafi spoke. "Anything new?"

His forearms still resting on the table, al-Rashad slowly raised his hands to his shoulders in a shrug and sticking out his bottom lip, turned his gaze from Rafi. Rafi placed his finger on one of the coins and scooted it to the center of the table. Al-Rashad snatched it up with lightning speed and plopped it back in the jar.

"Benjamin Flickermann has disappeared," he said in a raspy tone. Maylee realized that it was the first time in the entire encounter that she had heard him speak. His voice surprised her because it was quite strong and lucid in spite of how crazy he was. But he also sounded excited and far away, as if someone else were speaking through his lips.

Rafi registered the name. Benjamin Flickermann. An image came to his mind of a short, stout Jew who ran the little store ARTIFACTS. He dealt with antiques and paintings and the like.

"Why?" Rafi asked. The old man paused to scratch his neck with his yellow claws. Rafi pushed another coin forward and al-Rashad snatched it up.

"For a year they have been searching…" he was no longer looking at them but through them and his voice trailed off. Rafi sat unmoved and waited.

The old man shook his head and the cobwebs in his eyes cleared. "But," he began to laugh, "no one…can find it!" He grasped his belly with his hands and let silent laughter shake him. Wiping tears from his eyes, suddenly he became very sober. "Clever, clever, clever he was."

"Who?" Rafi asked, pumping him for details.

Al-Rashad lowered his brows into a deep scowl and all the muscles in his face grimaced. He rounded his lips and let out a sound of pity, followed by a *tisk tisk*. "But it is so interesting!" he said sincerely to Rafi, balling his hands into fists as if trying to hang on tightly to the information.

"The whole story," Rafi demanded as he set the crumpled bill in the middle of the table. Al-Rashad took the bill and rubbed it between his fingers, letting out a rancid sigh.

"They couldn't wait to get their hands on the money! All that money…" The thought of it made his wrinkled hands itch.

"They sold all of Kareem's things, of course," he added in afterthought, as if it were common knowledge.

"Who did?" Rafi asked.

The old man stopped fidgeting with the money and looked at him incredulously. "His sons. Haroun and Abdul." The old man paused to drink some water out of a filthy ceramic mug. He slammed it onto the rough wood and opened and closed his gnarled fist at Rafi, motioning for him to come closer.

"But, Kareem Hassan hid it!" he whispered, as if delighted at the secret. "Johann Barker has been looking for fifty years," he said dreamily, still gazing at the sheqel bill.

"What did he hide?' Rafi asked.

It took a moment for al-Rashad to hear the question, lost in his own thoughts. He began to laugh again, a smoky laugh that sounded almost like a cough. "That's just it!" he exclaimed. "No one knows what it is!"

"Who else wants it besides Johann Barker?" Rafi said.

Al-Rashad shrugged his shoulders as if that didn't matter. "No one," he said at first, shaking his head. "Everyone!" he added with a chuckle.

"But they think Benjamin Flickermann had it?" Rafi asked.

"Oh yes! Don't you see?" He jumped up again from his chair and grasped the front of Rafi's shirt, his knuckles white from the pressure. His eyes gleamed wildly as he peered into Rafi's face, so close their noses almost touched. He lowered his voice to a whisper and a dark secret floated on his sour breath. "Kareem only left one thing to his most beloved grandson, who in turn sold it to Benjamin Flickermann!"

He released Rafi and wilted back into his own chair, exhausted from the display. He shook his head sadly, as if he could warn the past. "That's why poor Benjamin had to die…"

"So he is dead?" Rafi asked, thinking of the body in the Garden. He was sure it was Benjamin Flickermann. But how many people knew he was dead?

Al-Rashad just shrugged his shoulders. His meaning was clear. If he wasn't already, he was about to be.

"Thanks, old friend," Rafi said to the old man, placing a strong hand on his bony shoulder. It was time to get out of there. Al-Rashad simply nodded and continued with his sad air as the three headed to the door.

Rafi's mind was racing. One thought was blaring loud enough to shut out the sounds of the Mahane Yehuda market. Kareem's grandson had unknowingly sold the greatest inheritance his grandfather could have left him! The mysterious Queen.

Amjad glowered at them as they appeared from the shadows. Obviously he was not amused with the game of hide-and-seek Rafi had led him on. Rafi ignored his glare and sauntered past him on the street, holding his head high. He had been on his own since he was thirteen, scratching a living off the streets and from his garden. He wasn't about to let someone tell him what to do now.

As Rafi placed one foot confidently in front of the other, he was quickly devising a plan. He had to get them to the Israel Museum. He knew someone there who could help them, a man who surely had information about the well-known Kareem Hassan. Life on the streets had taught Rafi to get what he needed; now, he used those same skills to get what he wanted. A twinkle played in his eyes as he wrapped the plan together. They would have to stop by his house first to pick up a few things if he was going to be successful.

TEN

Israel Museum

Maylee and Smith had just gathered in the kitchen to get permission to go to the museum when Uncle Arnold burst through the door. Smith instantly wriggled out from under his mom's arm and ran to his uncle.

He was the tallest man Maylee had ever seen. He had thick, curly hair and intensely dark eyes that always seemed to be squinting in a smile. She couldn't imagine anyone not getting along well with her uncle. Probably why he was so successful at running the Jewish-Arab hockey team in Jerusalem. Not an easy feat.

"It looks like you enjoyed the market!" he belted out. Uncle Arnold wrapped a strong arm around Smith's shoulders, squeezing him and playfully punching him until Smith laughed all of his breath out.

Amjad had entered with Uncle Arnold and stood awkwardly straight as he watched the interaction. He looked down at his long fingers and focused on shaping his cuticles. His shiny black hair was slicked down to his head and it shone in the morning sunlight that poured through the kitchen window. His eyes looked very tired, and for a moment, he reminded Maylee of a sea turtle.

Amjad was Uncle Arnold's right hand man for the interfaith hockey team Uncle Arnold sponsored, but he was so quiet, so not memorable that Maylee thought he could fade into the background in any room. Which is exactly what he did when Rafi popped his head in.

Rafi smiled coyly at Adah and pulled a handful of grapes from behind his back, stretching them out to her. "*Salam al-ykum.*"

"Well, hello to you too!" Adah greeted him, snatching the grapes from his hand and popping a bright green one into her mouth. She paused, mid bite, as she began to question the price of the gift. "Okay," she said, eying the boy suspiciously. "What do you want?"

His eyes sparkled with the knowledge that he had won the little game. "I was thinking Maylee and Smith really should see the Israel Museum," he said seriously. His face was stunningly innocent, as if he was genuinely concerned about his friends' cultural education.

Adah burst into a laugh, a beautiful laugh that started from the bottom of her lungs and rang out confidently. Rafi stood proudly, reveling in the cleverness of his invitation.

"Well," Adah began, wiping her hand on the red towel out of habit. "You should be bribing their mother, not me," she said, plucking another grape and tilting her head toward Carol. "But," she paused, lowering her voice and eying him with the air of an astute bargainer, "for some of your garlic olives, I might be able to put in a good word for you."

Rafi dropped his gaze and looked down sadly, kicking at the floor with the tip of his shoe as if lost in thought. He raised his eyes playfully and slowly reaching into his pocket, brought out a small jar of the cured fruit. He had researched his target well. Adah clapped her hands in joy and shooed the three of them toward the door while Carol smiled complacently.

"You have to take Amjad with you," Uncle Arnold interrupted, motioning with his head toward the young man everyone had forgotten was in the room. Amjad merely gave a slow nod that was almost a mix of a bow and a nod in one. Maylee turned her back to the rest of the group so that only Rafi could see her roll her eyes. He gave her a smug look and she knew exactly what it meant. They would find a way to ditch their companion. Again.

* * *

Rafi waved at the attendant at the museum through the glass as they approached the doors. He was thinking it wasn't so bad to have Amjad around this time, since he gave them a ride in Arnold's car. He missed the freedom of riding his scooter and not having to deal with Amjad, but with three people, the scooter was useless.

The attendant waved back and she greeted him in Arabic as the doors slid open. Rafi gave her a little nod and glancing around, hopped up onto the counter, swinging his legs.

"*Salam Alykam,* Ranya. How's my future wife?" he said with a wink. Ranya must have been at least thirty, but she still blushed slightly at the joke.

"*Salam Alykam.* You haven't been by in a while," she commented, glancing at the three others who stood slightly aloof from the two of them. "Busy, I see."

He shrugged. "You know, a little of this, a little of that. But, I felt a little sick today, that's actually why I'm here."

Ranya gave a motherly look and pressed a hand to his forehead. He leaned in and lowered his voice. "I had to see your pretty face; I think I'm lovesick!"

She laughed and playfully pushed him off the counter. "Take your friends and get out of here with that nonsense," she instructed. "Abraham will want to see you; he is in his workroom."

Rafi blew her a kiss and motioned for the others to follow him. He breezed through the halls with the air of someone who belonged there, not pausing to look at the art or the placards that gilded the walls. Pausing before a door, he turned and looked squarely at Amjad. "Go on and enjoy yourself," he said in a cordial and yet firm tone. "We'll catch up with you."

Amjad turned on his heel and walked away arrogantly, obviously perturbed. He wasn't too worried though. He had the keys to the car and the three would want a ride home at some point.

Rafi rapped lightly on the door, waited a moment, and then let himself in. The door opened into a sturdy room that felt more like a ship's cabin than an office. The floors were made of a golden wood that glowed in the heavy lamplight, and the walls were lined with shelves from top to bottom that held strange combinations. A stuffed cat bared his teeth on a shelf near the ceiling, as if he were guarding the tired books that leaned against one another on the surrounding shelves. A brain bobbed gently in a glass jar filled with liquid next to some dusty plastic flowers that seemed uncomfortably far from home.

Across the room from the entrance sat an old man at

a worn, wooden desk. Two long, gray curls framed his face and passed even his beard, which hung low on his belly. His ears twitched ever so slightly when they entered, but he made no other sign acknowledging their presence. Instead, he sat very still with his head down, concentrating hard on his hands. His lips moved without making a sound, and the silence became unbearable. Maylee shifted her weight between her left and right legs uncomfortably while Smith curiously eyed the brain out of the corner of his eye. He figured it would be rude to look directly at it.

Suddenly, the old man slapped his palms against the table and Maylee and Smith both jumped, startled. He got up, and the long black robe he wore made it seem as if he were gliding over the worn wood. "Well, well, well, my boy!" he said to Rafi in welcome, walking toward him with outstretched arms.

Rafi took one of his hands and bent to touch his forehead against the Rabbi's knuckles. The old man patted Rafi on the head, and grasping his shoulders, moved him to stand straight.

Abraham's bushy eyebrows lowered in a frown as he inspected Rafi's expression. "Something is bothering you. Come, sit down and let's talk."

ELEVEN

The Tale of the Queen

Rafi rested his elbows on the large table and leaned forward. There were no chairs, but rather a long bench that scooted up to the table, so Maylee and Smith sat on either side of him.

"Benjamin Flickermann is dead."

Abraham maintained his cool demeanor, but paused to swallow some lukewarm tea that was still on the table. He peered at him over the cup, his dark eyes glowing next to the green clay. "You're sure?"

Rafi nodded. "I saw his body."

The old man looked sad. He shook his head softly, and murmured a short prayer. There was a brief silence before Rafi spoke again.

"I wanted to ask you about something I overheard... really, the reason why Benjamin was killed. It has to do with Kareem Hassan."

The Rabbi caught his breath at the name and his spine visibly stiffened. Smith was uncomfortable with the conversation. He could feel the tension sweep through the room. Abraham breathed deeply and then nodded, an invitation to continue.

"The museum got a lot of Kareem's private collection when he died, right?"

"Yes, he willed a large portion to the museum. His sons sold the rest to us immediately."

Rafi leaned in closer and lowered his voice. "Rumor has it, Kareem left something of great value to one of his grandsons something the museum never had a chance to get their hands on. The young man sold it to Benjamin Flickermann at a fraction of its worth, but it was valuable enough to cost Benjamin his life."

"Go on," the Rabbi said, intrigued.

"Well, we happened to be in the Garden of Gethsemane a couple of nights ago." He waved away the Rabbi's questioning look and continued.

"We hid in the olive trees when we heard voices around midnight. Benjamin was already dead. They were looking for a place to bury him, but the soil at the Garden was too shallow so they headed to the old Jewish cemetery. We didn't stick around to see the end of the story, but we heard enough. At least two Americans and an Israeli believed Benjamin had something that was valuable enough to kill over."

"And what is this great treasure?"

"That's the thing; no one really knows," Rafi said, confused. He didn't tell Abraham about their visit to old al-Rashad. He was sure the Rabbi would disapprove of such a source. "They seemed to be talking in some sort of code. Maybe it will mean something to you."

Rafi licked his lips and swallowed hard. If Abraham didn't know, they were at a dead end. He scooted forward and reached across the table, resting his hand on Abraham's arm and looking intently into the old man's face. "They called whatever it was the Queen."

Abraham stopped breathing. The blood rushed from his face, leaving him a ghastly pale green. His hands gripped the table so hard his knuckles turned white. When he spoke, he could do no more than whisper. "What did you say?"

"The Queen, that's what they called it," Rafi repeated. "A fat American called Big Dale and an Israeli man with no accent. The Israeli is supposed to deliver it to him in a few days."

Abraham muttered in disbelief and threw his head back, staring at the ceiling. An awkward silence filled the room. Maylee and Rafi stared at the old man. Smith tried not to look at him or the brain, but he couldn't look anywhere without seeing one of them out of the corner of his eye. The Rabbi finally spoke. "So, it's true," he said in resignation.

The three friends waited expectantly for Abraham to offer an explanation. The old man's beard trembled as he spoke. "If the men who killed Benjamin are not mistaken, then this might be one of the greatest discoveries of the century!" He looked each of them squarely in the eye. They eyed him back uncertainly. He continued, "The tale is old, and the story begins over two thousand years ago, right here in Israel."

Abraham got up from the table and opened a cupboard, removing a map that had been rolled up. He opened it and spread it across the table, setting a book on each of its four corners to keep it flat. He pointed at Jerusalem, and drew his crooked finger westward, pausing at the banks of the

Dead Sea. A tiny dot labeled Qumran rested just above his fingernail. "This," he told them, "is where the story begins."

"In the winter of 1946, a young shepherd named Muhammad and his cousin, Jum'a, were with their flock right over here," he said pointing. "Near the Dead Sea. The boys were responsible to guide the sheep to food and water, and to keep them safe from predators, such as jackals and caracals."

Smith looked confused. "What's a caracal?"

"It's a wildcat with very pointy, black-tipped ears and big, round eyes. Sharp teeth and claws too," Abraham explained.

Smith nodded, satisfied.

"However," Abraham continued, "it's not just wild animals you have to be careful of when you are shepherding. Sheep are sweet, simple creatures, but they end up getting themselves into awkward situations. They learn to trust their person, and can recognize his voice and his face even years later. It's really the perfect job for any boy because…" Abraham winked at Smith and lowered his voice mysteriously. "There are lots of opportunities to go exploring outside!"

Smith's eyes sparkled and he smiled. Maybe the generation gap wasn't so wide here in Israel.

"You see, Jum'a was only fifteen that winter; he made games out of what seemed to be ordinary, day-to-day experiences and he let his imagination run wild among the sand-colored rocky paths and over the salty waves of the Dead Sea. You can imagine his excitement, then, when he found a secret enclosure."

Everyone in the room was fascinated with the prospect

of a secret chamber, even Abraham at his old age. Once, Maylee had stayed the night at a friend's house and they had discovered a laundry chute that they had used as a secret exit when Amy's brother had locked them in the room. A secret cave in the desert sounded even more intriguing.

"He had followed the nervous 'baa-baa' of one of his sheep that had wandered off from the rest of the herd, and found her caught with one leg wedged tightly, surrounded by rocks that had tumbled around her. The fluffy lamb gave a contented 'baa' in thanks as he released her, and she scurried up a little slope, as sheep tend to do when they are frightened."

Abraham paused, either because he was thirsty or because he wanted to build suspense. He took another sip of the now cold tea and carefully squared the cup, disguising a knot on the wooden table. He looked up, energy surging through his eyes.

"However, Jum'a didn't follow after her. As he was removing the stones, he had discovered the entrance to a deep cavern, an entrance big enough for a human to slip through."

The old man tapped his finger on his head as he spoke. "Now, Jum'a was as curious as a cat, but also very wise. He stopped to think before he acted." Abraham paused in his story and looked at each of his listeners separately, as if to teach them an important lesson. He was a Rabbi, after all.

"He knew that if the stones had hidden the entrance once, they could likely do it again, and he wasn't planning on dying undiscovered in some cave. He thought of his scarf that he used to keep the dust from his mouth and nose, and quickly untied it, leaving it tucked under a rock to mark the entrance to the cave."

Maylee and Smith looked at each other and grinned. They had been know to do those types of things.

Abraham continued. "The boy rushed after his sheep, and followed her back to where the rest of the flock was pleasantly grazing. His cousin Muhammad was playing a tune on a whistle he had carved out of wood. Breathlessly, Jum'a beckoned him to follow. As they ran, he told his cousin about his discovery. When they reached the cave they halted, peering into the inky blackness of the cave, but they could see nothing." As if on cue, the candle on Abraham's table flickered and burnt out, causing Maylee to shudder.

"Muhammad let out a shout and was greeted back by a throaty echo, the voice of the cavern bellowing back at him and eerily changing his voice. He threw in a rock to judge the size of the cave. Something shattered inside. The cousins decided to bring a lantern with them and explore the cave the next day."

Abraham paused. The three sat at rapt attention, waiting for him to continue. Abraham took a sip of tea and continued. "However, as they were walking back towards their flock, Jum'a heard a yelp from his cousin and turned just in time to see him disappear into the earth, as if the ground had swallowed him."

Smith gulped and looked at Abraham with big eyes. Abraham nodded at him.

"Muhammad had fallen through the thin crust of the earth into a cave, landing on broken shards and gashing his leg. Jum'a was able to pull out his bleeding cousin, who reached the daylight with something else in his hand." Abraham had closed his eyes and clasped his fist, as if he were actually there in that cave.

When he opened his eyes again, the lamplight danced in his dark pupils. "He held an ancient scroll that had been housed in an old ceramic jar—the very jar that he crushed in his fall and that had scraped him in return. It was a very old copy of the Old Testament book of Isaiah. He didn't realize it at the time, but he had stumbled upon one of the greatest religious discoveries ever made!"

"Wait... they just kept them in jars for who knows how long?" Maylee asked skeptically. That just didn't seem plausible.

"Yes," Abraham answered her, nodding energetically. "For over 2,000 years. It is almost unbelievable that they were so well preserved. You see, the people who lived at Qumran," he pointed to the map, "they hid their writings to save them from the Romans who probably would have burned them all."

"Hmm," Maylee grunted, thinking she would have tried to find a better way to keep her valuables safe.

"Anyways," Abraham continued, "the boys decided to see what else they might find in the cave, and slowly, Muhammad let himself back down. That day, they returned to their family with three scrolls. It was only a matter of time until the news spread; the oldest known preserved copies of the ancient Jewish texts had been discovered at the north shore of the Dead Sea—by two teenage shepherd boys."

In the moment of silence that followed, Maylee's stomach growled loudly. She grasped her belly with her hands and looked embarrassed. Smith and Rafi chuckled and she sent them a chilling glare. Abraham was more gracious. "Let's pause and have a snack," he offered. Everyone agreed.

He made tea from a little water pitcher that plugged into the wall, and took some more clay cups from one of his many cupboards. He offered them each a pear, some almonds, and a little slice of cheese. Smith thought that was a way better snack than peanut butter and jelly sandwiches.

No one talked while they ate, but the quiet didn't make anyone uncomfortable. They were all processing the information. Smith was imagining what he would do if he got caught in a dark cave, and he shuddered when he thought about the pointy-eared caracals that roamed through the desert.

Rafi was the first to break the silence. "So, where does Kareem Hassan come into the picture?"

Abraham sucked the core of his pear and tossed it in the trash. Wiping his hands on his robe, he began again. "Kareem started working for the museum in the late 1950s. There were three of us, myself included, who worked closely with the scrolls before and after the Six Day War between Jordan and Israel. That was in 1967. The scrolls transferred from Jordan's possession to Israel's possession when Israel won, and the scrolls were transferred here to the Israel Museum." He spread his hands out toward the walls of the museum.

"During the time, more scrolls were being discovered and painstakingly put back together, as most of them had fallen apart. It was hard to document which was which and who it belonged to and a hundred other questions. But, when we were unpacking the scrolls here at the museum, we smelled a rat. Something just wasn't right after the transfer, but we couldn't put a finger on it. When the scrolls were pieced together completely, it was discovered that there was an interesting gap in the history."

The Rabbi reached under his desk and pulled out a copy of the Holy Scriptures. He turned a couple of very thin pages and found the index. He turned it so the others could see and ran his finger down the list. "You see, in part or in whole, every book of what is considered the Holy Scriptures is represented in these scrolls, except for one." He paused dramatically about half way down the list. His finger shook. From age? Excitement? Probably a combination of both. "Not a word of the book of Esther ever surfaced after the transfer."

Abraham got up from the table and opened a cabinet. Inside, there was a squat black safe which he opened with a combination. Taking out a moleskin book, he returned to the table. The book was closed with a locking clasp, the key to which hung around his neck on a gold chain. He unlocked it, and caressed the worn exterior lovingly before he opened it.

"A lifetime of memories are here," he said slowly, and a sad smile played on his lips. "The joys and fears of an old man are remembered in these pages; the things that mattered most. It talks of lies, deceit, and hate. And love." He looked at them the way old people look at young people—as if he wished he still had his youth, but that the thought of living it all again made him very tired.

"I was only eighteen when I got an internship at the museum. Handling the scrolls was considered tedious work, so they put three of us young ones to work on that. Kareem and I were a part of that team. In this book, I kept my own private documentation of what we were seeing pass through. I knew the Dead Sea Scrolls were going to be big before most of the world even knew that they existed." Abraham smiled to himself, drifting off to a place hidden in his memory. His eyes were still far away when he spoke again.

"We made a game of the boring work, you see. It may have been a little sacrilegious, but we gave nicknames to all the Old Testament books so we could talk about them in public without compromising the museum's privacy policy. Genesis, for example, we called 'my big sister;' to talk about Exodus, we would start with 'last time I went on a trip...'"

He looked each of them in the eye hard and stopped at Rafi. His voice faltered, but his gaze did not. "Esther, you see, we had nicknamed 'The Queen.'"

"Oh, wow," Rafi thought aloud running his hands through his hair. "This is a big deal."

Abraham nodded. "If Kareem really had The Queen and left it to someone in his family and word got out, it's a treasure beyond price. To be sure, it will be bought at nothing less than the price of blood." It was that serious.

"Whether it is real or not, the idea itself was enough to get Benjamin Flickermann killed," Rafi commented.

"Exactly," Abraham agreed. "But, I have a hunch it is real." He opened his moleskin book to almost the very beginning.

"You see," he said, turning the book so they could see it, "once upon a time, I saw the manuscript. I wondered if I was crazy or had imagined it, because I never saw it again." They looked down to read what he was showing them in the book. On the page, a much younger Abraham had written: April 19, 1966—first glance at a Queen.

Abraham had told them all he knew, and the conversation was nearly over. He sent them away with a last piece of advice and a warning. "You have information only two other people and I ever knew. The secret has somehow been leaked, and the fact that you know about it puts you all in danger." He looked at them very seriously. "Be careful, and be wise."

As he said this, he tapped his finger against his head just as he had done while talking about Jum'a and Muhammad in the story. The three nodded at him gravely.

Rafi had his hand on the handle to open the door when he suddenly turned to ask the Rabbi one last question. "You said there were three of you on the Dead Sea Scrolls team, three who knew about The Queen. Who is the other person besides you and Kareem Hassan?"

The ice in Abraham's heart seemed to freeze his gaze. His eyes narrowed as he spit out a name like it was poison on his tongue. "The third man is Johann Barker."

TWELVE

A Trip to the Dead Sea

They had to get to the caves. That was where this started, after all. Maylee didn't think it would be a problem. How could their mom argue when they were supposed to be touring the Holy Land anyways? They decided to let Smith ask. He winked at them through long lashes.

"I got this," he said with a smile as Amjad dropped them back off at the house. They waved goodbye to Rafi who trotted into his house next door.

Carol and Adah were sipping tea when they got inside. The windows were open and a breeze wafted lazily through the room. Carol looked up at her children and smiled for once. Maybe Aunt Adah was rubbing off on her a little.

Smith and Maylee's tummies rumbled and the smell of dinner made them realize how hungry they were. The snack from Abraham had only tided them over for a little bit.

"Your Uncle will be home any minute," Adah told them. "Go wash up. And Maylee? Would you and Smith please set the table?"

Maylee nodded at her aunt, and brother and sister raced down the hall to the bathroom. They came back into the kitchen with wet shirts and looked guiltily at their Aunt

Adah who raised an eyebrow. "My bathroom better not have water all over it." Smith hurried back down the hall to clean it up while Maylee set the table.

Smith heard the front door open and close, jingling keys settling on their nail in the wall. Uncle Arnold was home. When Smith finished drying the bathroom, he found them all seated at the table and waiting for him. "There's the man of the hour!" His uncle winked at him and mussed his hair. "Smith, why don't you lead us in prayer."

Smith nodded. "Great God," he began, "thanks for our food and our family and that we get to be here in Israel." He opened one eye to make sure they were all quiet and concentrated, and decided to drop the bomb. "I pray that while we are here in Israel we can go see the caves where the Bible was found. In Jesus' name, Amen."

He was grinning with his own eyes wide open, clearly proud of himself when everyone unfolded their hands and opened their eyes. He held his fork in one hand and his spoon in the other and looked around the table. Maylee smacked her head with her hand and shook her head. She didn't think he was very sly.

The adults, however, were taken in by his feigned innocence. Adah's eyes sparkled and she looked at her husband. "That's great that he is interested in the history," she commented. She passed a green salad around the table and scooped some onto Smith and Maylee's plates alongside a chicken breast and some brown rice. Uncle Arnold nodded in agreement. "Amjad's cousin actually works there," he said between bites. "I'll see if we can head over there in the morning and spend the day. What do you think, sis?"

Carol nodded. "Sure, maybe we can float in the Dead Sea while we are there!"

Maylee set her fork down loudly and rolled her eyes. "Eew mom, that sounds nasty. We aren't zombies."

"You know why they call it that, right?"

Maylee shook her head, a look of disgust still on her face.

"It's called the Dead Sea because the water is so salty that nothing can survive. But, it's the salt in the water that makes it super easy to float in. You can actually sit up in the water and read a book if you want!"

Smith poked at his rice. He had spent years at swimming lessons and now he was fearless of the water. But everyone knew he still freaked out when he tried to lay on his back and stick out his stomach to float across the pool. He wondered how anyone could possibly sit up and stay afloat.

Uncle Arnold nodded. "It's true," he agreed. "We can't go over there and not experience the Dead Sea."

Adah held a glass in her hand, but paused to point at Maylee and Smith before drinking. "That's not water you will want to splash each other with, though," she said to her niece and nephew. "Get it in your eyes and it will be miserable. Swallow too much of that salty water and you will be throwing up on the beach and it won't be a fun experience."

"Do you think we could invite Rafi?" Maylee asked as she looked at her plate, focusing a little too hard on a piece of lettuce.

Adah looked at her husband with the same question in her eyes.

"Sure, he is like part of the family," Uncle Arnold said.

Smith pulled his fist to his stomach in victory and let out a "Yes!" With excitement, Maylee and Smith rushed through the kitchen with their plates and asked to be excused to go invite their friend. They bounded up the stairs, preferring to crawl over their balcony and down the grapefruit tree into his yard rather than the more traditional enter-through-the-front-door routine.

"Go ahead and invite him for breakfast in the morning too," Adah called out after them, laughing merrily. She turned to Carol with a smile. "I'm so glad to see them happy here, making friends in my country. They will be speaking Arabic before you know it, hanging out with Rafi." *Kids see no color or culture at that age,* she thought wistfully.

Maylee flew onto the balcony and over the wall. "Rafi! They're taking us!" she called breathlessly. She dropped into the little orchard next door and found Rafi waiting for her. "We get to explore the secret of the caves and the missing scroll!"

Rafi's eyes sparkled as he thought again of the caves where ancient secrets had lain hidden for thousands of years. He had, of course, already scoured the area fruitlessly time after time, hoping that he would find another script overlooked by archaeologists and bounty hunters. Still, his blood pulsed hot through his veins as he thought of the lottery prospect of a historical discovery. And, of course, a renewed hope that they might find out more about The Queen.

They were leaving early the next morning. In twelve hours, they would be on their way to the caves of Qumran. That night, the three friends lay awake in their dark houses, waiting for the day to finally come to life.

THIRTEEN

Dr. Davis Calls Back

The sound of his ringing phone woke him. Sort of. His mind was foggy and his tongue felt thick and heavy. *The sleeping pill,* he thought. The drug must have slowed his responses because the phone was still ringing and he had yet to answer it. He stretched to the table and knocked his cell phone on the ground. It still rang threateningly. He snatched it up and answered.

"Hello?"

"Hassan?" The voice was high-pitched and whiny, but sharp.

"Speaking."

"Hadassah, huh?" she asked smugly. "Glad I could be such an influence."

Now he was awake!

"Took you long enough to call, Francine," he grumbled.

"It's Dr. Davis to you, Jerome. And I haven't been in Israel the past few days."

"Where have you been, exactly?"

"Vacationing. With a very good alibi. I think you know why. By the way, where were you on the night of June 16?"

He could hear the laughter in her voice and he hated

her for it. She was playing this like it was a joke. And Benjamin had been his friend.

"I'll buy your next vacation ticket to Hell, and you can have all the demons you want for alibis," he spit at her.

"Tisk, tisk, Jerome. Are you threatening me?" Her voice was playful, but dripping with challenge.

"I have your precious Queen," he said, steering the conversation.

He could hear her sharp intake of air.

"You have it?" she whispered.

"Yes. All nicely tucked away and safe where no one will find it." It was his turn to play with her.

"How is it?" she asked, excitement in her voice. Was her tone hopeful? Fearful? Impatient? He needed her impatient. *Draw it out a little longer,* he thought. *Build the suspense until she just can't take it.*

He sighed, a long breath escaping from his lips. He decided to chide her. "Oh, Francine…this is why you really should call people back, you know."

"Just answer the question! How is she?" she barked.

"Lovely," he said, letting the word slide off his tongue. He laughed sharply, "You really should see it, you know. Veiled for over two thousand years to the eyes of all but my grandfather. And now mine, of course."

He imagined the greed rising in her stomach and heating her. "And, just think," he continued. "In a few days, she will be all yours!"

He paused, letting her bask in the thought before he tugged at her jealous strings again. "Until then, I'm quite enjoying her company. Oh, now don't get upset," he soothed her, "just a peek here and there."

"That's mine!" she said darkly. "I don't want you looking at it or getting your grimy hands all over it!" She was yelling now. "You don't have the slightest idea how to handle such a treasure!"

Jerome said nothing, but smiled to himself. This is exactly where he wanted her. Mad, angry, and fuming with jealous rage. Irrational. He knew it was scratching her now, clawing at her. She had to get it, no matter the cost, just so that he couldn't have it.

"I'm taking her with me today," he chirped. "A little journey home for one last visit. The feeling that she will be back in the caves, still wearing her disguise thrills me."

"You wouldn't dare!"

"Try me!" he taunted, hanging up the phone.

Francine nearly wet herself, she was so upset. The man was actually enjoying toying with her. *No one,* she thought, *NO ONE hangs up on Dr. Francine Davis!* She poured the rest of her coffee down the sink and called Jenny Pruitt.

"Cancel everything today," she commanded. "And schedule me a trip to Qumran. The earliest tour possible."

FOURTEEN

Smith Slips Up

Although the trip to Qumran wasn't more than thir-ty miles, Uncle Arnold had suggested they travel by bus. They chose a trip which would also gain them a guided tour of the area as well as lunch and a dip in the Dead Sea. Maylee, Smith, and Rafi decided to sit at the far back of the bus to give themselves some distance from the adults, making it easier to discuss the events of the previous days without being overheard.

"I hardly slept at all last night," admitted Maylee. "I kept on hearing strange sounds and imagining that Big Dale had tracked us back to the house, looking for the scroll."

"Me either," interjected Smith. "I kept thinking I could hear the swish swishing of a ghost in a jogging suit on the balcony," he declared, his eyes large and serious.

"Let's discuss what we know so far," Rafi suggested, closing his eyes in thought. "Kareem died, leaving the most precious part of his inheritance to his grandson. The grand-son didn't know what it was, or didn't value it, so sold it to Benjamin Flickermann.

"A man named Johann Barker, who just so happened to work with Abraham and Kareem back in the day, is looking for it. Benjamin ends up murdered by the Big Dale, Jack, and Jerome. They still don't know where it is."

"As far as that goes, neither do we!" added Maylee.

"What I don't understand," interjected Smith, "is how Big Dale, Jack, and Jerome found out about the scroll."

Rafi frowned, deep in thought. Smith had an excellent point. How did they know about the scroll, a secret that was only privy to three old men, one of which was now dead?

"Remember what old al-Rashad said? He said that Johann Barker has been looking for something since Kareem died." Rafi lowered his voice to a whisper. "The way I see it, there are three options. One, Kareem told someone else about it. Two, the guys in the garden are actually working for Johann Barker. Three, Johann let the secret slip while he was searching."

"Well," announced Smith, "I think we are ahead of the game. At least we know that what they are looking for is called The Queen!"

As Smith was speaking, the bus took a sharp turn and an old man making his way to the bathroom nearly fell into them. He smiled apologetically and continued shuffling into the tiny water closet.

As soon as the old man had stepped past them, Rafi gripped Smith's arm firmly, causing him to grimace. "Do not ever repeat that phrase in public again," he said with a warning. "It is enough to get you killed! We shouldn't even be talking about this here. No more discussion until we are back safe at your uncle's house. We are here. Time to leave the bus."

Smith tried to keep the tears from welling up in his

eyes. He hadn't meant for the outburst, he had just been so excited from figuring out how The Queen's secret name had surfaced. He hung behind briefly, fidgeting with his sweatshirt and attempting to cover how badly his feelings were hurt.

Maylee gave him a quick squeeze on his arm and whispered, "Chin up! No one on this bus cares about the discussion of a few kids. I'm sure they didn't think anything of it. Rafi just is used to having to be really careful."

Smith gave her a grateful smile, but he was still hurt. He found his mom and tucked himself under her arm and walked in silence, staring at the floor as the group exited the bus and entered the tourism center. They had ten minutes until the tour started, so Smith decided to escape to the bathroom to splash a little cold water on his face and get himself back together.

Rafi followed him. He looked coldly at himself in the mirror. Apologizing wasn't something he did. Ever. He glanced at Smith who stood at the sink next to him. His soft eyes brimmed with tears. Rafi sighed. He wanted to make sure they were good.

Rafi wet his hands and let the cool water run over his face as well. He dried his hands and ruffled Smith's blond hair as their eyes caught in the mirror above the sinks. "We're cool, Smith. Don't even worry about it."

Smith forced a wary smile.

"Stay close by me during the tour," Rafi whispered, his eyes glittering with a secret. "I have my own tour we will take and they will never know we were gone!"

FIFTEEN

Inside the Caves

The tour started under a giant umbrella in the heart of the Essene settlement at Qumran. The tour guide was a petite older woman with fire-red hair who looked better suited to serve cookies out of a country kitchen. "Don't get lost or fall behind the pack," she warned her group. She sounded every inch as Scottish as she was. "It could be another two thousand years before you are discovered down in these caves!"

A little girl with pink flowers printed on her dress looked at her smugly and rolled her eyes. The woman took her up on the challenge. She leaned in toward the little girl and said poignantly, "And from what I hear, shepherding is becoming a lost art."

The little girl shrunk away from the guide as the warning sunk in; it could literally be two thousand years before anyone found her if she got lost.

Maylee smiled to herself. She liked this witty woman whose voice was larger than her stature. She was also thankful that the guide had scared the little girl into sticking close to her father. None of them wanted her lagging behind and messing up Rafi's plan to show them his own tour once things got started.

"I found the secret a few years back," he whispered to them. "I was twelve at the time. Back when my uncle was still alive."

Rafi tipped his head to the right, motioning for them to lag back, feigning interest in a placard that marked where the shepherd boy, Muhammed, had fallen into the first cave and discovered the first three scrolls. "I paused here and didn't know that the tour had moved on," he said. "I could almost hear the 2,000 year-old echo of hurried footsteps running across the rocks and sand. I imagined the Essenes searching for crevices in which to hide their sacred manuscripts from the hands of the Romans that had already destroyed Jerusalem and who were galloping towards Qumran."

Smith and Maylee peered over the rocks and looked into the vastness of the now unpopulated territory. They could almost hear it too. Rafi tucked himself behind a mound of white dirt and the others followed. They could hear the crunch of feet on the blanched rocks fade as the tour moved away from them.

Rafi's voice sounded loud when he spoke again. "All of a sudden, I was alone. The other voices had disappeared, and I didn't want to get lost out here like another speck of sand in the desert. I picked my way around this crumbling wall," he said, guiding them and thinking aloud, "then turned left into a half-collapsed corridor."

They walked as he spoke. "I was listening hard for the voice of the guide, but ended up in a huge cave!" He described the cave to them, telling them about the clay pots he had found stacked on some old wooden shelves. He remembered the room as being dim, lit by some sort of fire lantern.

"I just pray I can find the same cavern again," he said, almost to himself.

Maylee and Smith followed him carefully, as though one wrong step and they would share Muhammed's fate and fall into a cave. Rafi paused, pondering the route he had taken. He remembered that the cavern appeared to have only one entrance, but that he had actually heard voices drifting through a second opening.

He surveyed the land and decidedly set upon his path. He stopped confidently at the mouth of a high, arid enclosure. They had arrived at the same cavern with the tall ceiling and flickering lantern that Rafi had stumbled upon during his visit years before. Rafi's ears perked up and he put his finger to his lips in a shushing motion, stopping short of entering the room.

A cloud of smoke wafted lazily out of the crevice and curiously inspected the eyes and noses of the three explorers before disappearing into the bright day. Hushed voices in the cave quivered with nervous excitement and rose in an escalated disagreement.

"What were you thinking?" a deep voice growled.

"I thought it would be safe to bring it here!" a man began. "I had no idea he would be here today!"

"You should have just followed the plan!" the first voice hissed.

"Your plans don't exactly work out smoothly." A tinge of challenge heated his words.

One voice didn't bother to whisper. "That's quite enough you idiots! Give it to me!" she said in a mocking tone, slapping her hands together definitively.

"The solution is simple," she decided. "Leave it here where no one will find it, and I will come back after the caves are closed to recover it. Leave something else while you're at it." She paused, and Rafi imagined her to be scanning the room.

A woman yelped, half in pain, half in shock. "That ought to do it," the voice continued. "A woman missing a diamond earring from her husband is a good cover in case anyone should happen along. Jerome, you will accompany me, of course. Now go," she commanded as if she was beginning to get bored with her companions.

Maylee, Smith, and Rafi crouched along the side of the swollen earth, desperately trying to hide in a shadow, but the stark sun blazed relentlessly. The pitter-patter of quiet footsteps echoed through the darkness and disappeared to the other side of the hill.

But there was still a presence in the secret chamber. The sound of high heels scraped along the stone floor and paused. They could hear her still talking as she walked.

"This is what you get for trying to take matters into your own hands," she lectured. "You are lucky that my Queen is still safe, or you wouldn't live to see the sunrise tomorrow."

A dull rattle proceeded from the room as someone removed a clay jar from its wooden shelf. Almost as quickly, the jar was replaced back in its space of repose and the heels scratched confidently towards the other exit. Her voice faded away, still scolding Jerome for putting The Queen in danger.

Smith and Maylee let out tense sighs as the sounds disappeared into the depths of the caves. Rafi led them into the room as the sound of the footsteps became hollow and far away.

Immediately, they searched the clay pots. Rafi was the tallest, and so he searched the highest shelf he could reach. Maylee began on the opposite side, working towards Rafi. Smith paused and contemplated, rather than joining directly into the search.

A woman who wears heels in a cave in the middle of the desert... he thought. *She's probably going to pick the easiest jar to get to.*

He glanced at the clay vessels that would be a little lower than shoulder height to his mom. He stepped forward and peered in one jar that was slightly forward. Empty.

Maylee tapped Rafi on the shoulder. She held up a brilliant jewel that danced like fire as it caught the light from the torch. He looked at it greedily and nodded when she placed it in the side pocket of her jeans.

Smith looked in the containers on either side of the squat jar that was out of place. Maybe the woman in heels had moved it when she scooted the other jar back. *Bingo!* he thought, as his hands touched something soft. He dug deep into the clay pot, snatching out a package wrapped in thick plastic.

Just as Maylee and Rafi crowded around the package, they heard voices approaching from the secondary entrance. Left with no choice, Smith clutched the package to his chest and they darted from the cave, back into the harsh sunlight that bored down on them like a spotlight. This time, they didn't wait to eavesdrop, but quickly retraced their steps, scurrying like mice over the rocky terrain.

Rafi led them around an old cistern where they slowed to catch their breath. They could see their tour group again, and they managed to tuck into the back of the crowd as the group rounded a corner. Smith hung back and hastily strapped the package to his waist with his belt. He had brought a sweatshirt to use as a pillow and untying it from his waist, he tossed it on in spite of the warm day, covering the bulging package.

Their group passed quietly by the other side of the secret cave, and Maylee elbowed Rafi in the ribs. They glanced cautiously at the wall that masterfully hid the secret room only feet away from them on this side. Not a sound came from the interior. Either the intruders had already left, or they were waiting for the tour to pass by. Maylee's heart slowed a little back in the security of the pack, but Smith spent the rest of the tour scanning the crowd for an American woman in heels.

The tour ended, and everyone paused to use the restroom in the gift shop and wash up before lunch on the shores of the Dead Sea. Out of the glass windows, they could see the workers from *SEE ISRAEL* setting up a small picnic area about a hundred yards from the entrance. The thirty-some visitors began filtering out the door and towards the beach.

Maylee, Smith, and Rafi exited together and a friendly voice called after them, "Thanks so much! I hope you enjoyed the tour!" Maylee turned and waved to a short Israeli man who stood grinning at them behind the counter.

As they settled down in a remote spot away from the chattering crowd, Smith was pensive and silent. The plastic stuck uncomfortably to his sweating stomach. Carol and

Adah opted to float in the Sea after trying in vain to coax the kids to join them. Adah looked suspiciously at Smith. "It's 85 degrees out here, take that ridiculous sweatshirt off."

Smith just rested his head on Maylee's shoulder and shook his head *no*. Adah touched his cheek with the back of her hand. "You don't feel like you have a fever," she stated. "You need some rest, it's been a long day. Don't even ask me to stay up late tonight," she warned as she left them and moved toward the water.

When she was out of earshot, Maylee and Rafi urged him to guess what was in the package, but he looked at them, pale, and with a fearful calm in his eyes.

"Didn't you notice?" he asked. Maylee and Rafi returned his gaze with a blank expression. "The man who works for the tour company, the one who told us goodbye...he doesn't have the Israeli accent!"

SIXTEEN

Disappointment

The ride on the bus back to Jerusalem was nearly silent. Several of the adults had dozed off after their late lunch, while Maylee and Smith listened to their iPods. Rafi stared out the window, his thoughts rushing through his mind as quickly as the bus shot through the countryside.

Everyone was tired by the time they got home. Carol took a book to her room and said goodnight after helping Adah clean up after dinner. Arnold fell asleep in his chair in the living room before the news even went on. Adah sat quietly working on a puzzle, pausing only long enough to yawn several times.

Maylee and Smith were the only ones who weren't tired. Fueled by curiosity and adrenaline, they were anxious to examine the package that was still strapped around Smith's waist. "Rafi wanted to show us something after dinner," Maylee told her aunt.

Adah looked at her and sighed. "I already said don't ask, Maylee. Today has been a long day, and I don't want you or Smith getting sick," she said, thinking of Smith's strange behavior hours before at the banks of the Dead Sea.

Maylee looked dejected. "We aren't gonna get sick," she

began. Turning from the table defeated, she let out an angry huff and muttered, "It's not like everyone in this house is as old as you are."

Adah heard her. She could feel her temper boiling her blood and strangling the compassion she had worked so hard to grow in her spirit. A thousand stabs came to mind, but she controlled her tongue. *Breathe,* she thought, *you are the adult here. Imagine you were in her shoes, in a foreign country on vacation with a cute older boy next door who wanted to spend time with you...*

That calmed her a little bit. She always had been quite the romantic. *Imagine if your father had left you, wouldn't you want to live any chance at happiness in the moment, afraid that tomorrow it might be gone?* The compassion was back and breathing.

She got up from her puzzle and went to sit next to her niece. "Hey," she said.

"Hmm?" Maylee grunted, staring at the floor rather than look at her aunt.

"How long did you plan on staying over there?"

Maylee shrugged and rolled her eyes before she finally answered. "I don't know; not that late."

Adah sighed. "Maylee," she began, pausing to organize her words. "You are getting older, and it's okay to express what you want. But part of being adult is learning to be diplomatic about it. When you get an attitude, it makes me feel like you are tired and I shouldn't let you go."

Maylee sat listening to her but not looking at her, her lips pursed and her eyes narrow.

"Plus," Adah said poking her niece playfully, "never take a stab at a woman's age and expect to get what you want!"

Maylee laughed with her and grabbed her hands. She looked up at her aunt and Adah saw so many emotions there. Pain and excitement. Lust for life. Worry. She wanted to wrap her up in a thick blanket and protect her from the world. But Maylee was like a butterfly struggling to get out of its cocoon. Too long in the cocoon or too much help getting out would stunt her growth forever.

Adah reached out and smoothed her hair. Maylee wouldn't admit it, but she craved that attention. There was so much love in her aunt's touch. Love that Maylee hadn't felt in a long time.

"Go over, but both of you be back by ten. I want you to get home and get ready for bed without any arguing or complaining. Deal?"

"Deal!"

Maylee jumped up and called to Smith who was watching TV. He leapt off the floor and they hurried up the stairs and over the balcony. Rafi was waiting for them. He looked around, and decided it was safer to invite them inside.

They hadn't been in Rafi's house before. It was overly simple and very small. It had a bathroom, a closet, and a kitchen that connected to the only room in the house. Smith was looking around for the bedroom, but he finally realized there wasn't one. This was it. Rafi had no furniture, except a large cushion and a low table. There were several baskets stacked against the wall and he grabbed three of them. Turning them over, he sat on one and motioned for Maylee and Smith to sit on the other two.

"Where is your family?" Smith asked before he took his sweatshirt off.

"It's just me."

The silence that followed was awkward. They didn't know he didn't have a mom or dad, and Maylee suddenly felt guilty for being so selfish. Rafi didn't seem to mind.

"Let's check out this package," he urged.

Smith took off his sweatshirt and unstrapped his belt, slowly removing the parcel. His stomach itched where the plastic had stuck all day, irritating his delicate skin.

Smith took off several layers of plastic to reveal a light-weight, aluminum cylinder—slightly larger than a Pringles can—with little straps like a backpack. He took the top off, and the three of them held their breath as he removed a rolled-up item. Smith turned to Maylee, and she grasped one end the canvas while Smith gently began to unroll from the end he held.

The three were surprised and disappointed when it opened up to reveal a poorly done rectangular painting. It looked as though the image had been printed onto the canvas, and then sloppily covered with paint. It was a giant red flower, waking up and unfolding in the morning hours with a bee buzzing, anxiously waiting to gather some pollen.

The three sat in silence, unsure what to think or say. Maylee was the first to cut through the quiet. "I just don't get what the big deal is over this ugly painting," she began. "It's clearly a print, and it doesn't even have the artist's signature on it."

The deception hit Rafi hard. He had really believed they were on to something. He shook his head in silence. He let out a dejected sigh and shrugged his shoulders. "We fell for a decoy."

"But, we heard them talking about it in the secret chamber," Maylee countered.

"That whole argument was probably staged. They planted a fake, maybe even more than one." Rafi looked like someone had socked him in the gut. He felt so foolish. "The real Queen is still in their hands, and there is nothing we can do about it."

The resignation in his voice frightened Smith. So, they were just going to give up? Defiance rose up in his chest. Benjamin Flickermann deserved more than that.

Rafi stood. He needed some space. The disappointment was suffocating him. Maybe a drink would help him breathe. "I'm going to get a glass of water, want something?" he asked his friends. They both shook their heads in a silent no.

Smith sat, gazing at the canvas. "What if we missed something?" he said. "What if this is really valuable for some reason, and we just can't see it?"

"No," Rafi said sadly, kneeling next to Smith and patting him on the forearm in a hopeless gesture. "This is garbage. No one on the street would pay anything for this. I'm sorry, my friends. This is no Queen, merely an imposter."

A dejected Smith and Maylee returned back to Uncle Arnold's neighboring house at 9:30. Adah greeted them in disbelief that they were so early when their curfew wasn't for another thirty minutes. Maylee mumbled an excuse about being tired, and she and Smith scurried to the room they were sharing, anxious to be away from her curious eyes.

Maylee turned her iPod on and crawled into her bed facing the wall. Sadness for Rafi and disappointment over

The Queen had put her into one of her moods, and she didn't want to see or talk to anyone, even Smith.

The feeling was mutual. Smith waited until her breathing became deep and regular, signaling that she had fallen asleep. It seemed like forever. He crawled out of bed with the art case and slipped into the closet. Shutting the door, he tugged on a thin string that hung from the ceiling and illuminated a single, dull light bulb.

He popped the top off of the canister and took out the rolled up canvas, setting it on the floor by his side. Carefully, he began to inspect the inside of the aluminum can with his fingers, hoping to find something. *A switch,* he thought, *or perhaps a secret key or note stuck inside that would reveal the location of the true Queen.* He searched for a long time, refusing to believe their failure, but in vain.

He scrutinized the painting one last time before letting it roll itself up loosely. The edges of the canvas were flimsy and there was a thick, yellowing stain where it must have been glued to the back of a frame. The border was too big for the painting anyway, as if the artist had only painted the middle of the picture and not bothered with the rest.

Smith tried hard to see something special in the piece, but he knew enough about art to recognize that it was worthless. This was no undiscovered *Mona Lisa.*

Exceptional art wasn't something that could be defined in words, he knew. It just felt right, like taking a shot on the basketball court and knowing it was going to swish through the net before it even left your fingertips.

It was the perfect combination of imperfections that made it beautiful—the way dying flowers smell the sweetest

and the way disturbing a quiet lake causes ripples to mul-
tiply the reflection of sunlight. Smith could feel art before
he even really looked at it, the way he could wake up in
the morning and just know it had snowed in the night before looking out the window. He knew this piece wasn't any
good.

He clicked the light off in the closet and slowly, crept
back into his bed. The last thing he wanted to do was fall
asleep curled up in the closet. Maylee would make fun of
him; she would probably tell Rafi and they would laugh at
him in secret, thinking he had been scared. Smith didn't
want that.

Something about the older boy inspired him, making
him want to be strong, independent, and grown-up like Rafi
with his responsibilities and freedoms. He didn't have any
parents, and he was still okay.

Smith opened the canister and was going to put the
painting back in it when an idea occurred to him. Feeling
his way around the nightstand between his and Maylee's
beds, he grabbed the *faux* scroll of Isaiah that his mom had
bought him at the gift shop that day. He rolled it up and
placed it in the aluminum can, re-wrapping it in the plastic
covering. It was a way cooler presentation for his scroll, he
thought.

And besides, something just wasn't sitting right with
him about that painting. He stuck the painting under his
pillow and held it with one hand, lying on his stomach.
He couldn't quite put his finger on it, but he knew he had
missed something when he had scrutinized the canvas and
container.

He tossed and turned that night in his sleep, dreaming of a mute Benjamin Flickermann who merely pointed at the canvas and looked intently at Smith, commissioning him to discover its secret. His fitful sleep lead him to sleep late, and when he finally woke up, he realized something was wrong.

SEVENTEEN

Smith Comes Clean

His heart was racing, and he had been dreaming that someone was chasing him through an alley on a hot Jerusalem night. He was sweating hard, so he kicked the covers off. He calmed as he realized that he was safe in Uncle Arnold's house. The sun streamed through the windows and he looked around the room. Maylee was no longer in her bed, and he was surprised that she hadn't tortured him awake like she normally did. *She is probably hanging out with Rafi, visiting old al-Rashad or following a new lead about The Queen!* he thought angrily, hopping to his feet.

At that moment, a quiet knocking sounded at the door. Uncle Arnold peered his head in. "Good morning!" he said softly, "mind if I come in?" He turned, closing the door without waiting for a response. Smith sat back down, making a space for Uncle Arnold to sit at the base of the bed as well.

"I didn't let Maylee wake you this morning," he began. "I feel that there is something we need to talk about, man to man."

Oh, great... Smith thought, feeling suddenly guilty. He immediately tensed up and glanced at his pillow to see if the painting was peeping out from underneath. He let out a silent breath of relief to see that it was still safely hidden.

Uncle Arnold proceeded, "I'm not impressed at you guys ditching Amjad. Especially twice." He put his hands up as Smith's jaw dropped and eyes opened wide. "No, don't try to deny it or make any excuses," he said.

"I sent Amjad along to look after you, to make sure you were safe. Your disrespecting him is indirectly a sign of disrespect to me. How that makes me feel should be obvious," he said with a stern look. "I didn't get to be where I am at in life because I'm dumb. I know you kids are up to something, suddenly interested in museums and historical discoveries. I would rather you tell me now than make me figure it out. But one way or the other, I'm going to know."

They sat in silence for a moment. Smith stared at his toes. He had nothing to say. They weren't doing anything wrong! They were actually trying to help. And Abraham had told them to be careful, that the secret they had wasn't meant to be shared.

Uncle Arnold sighed. "It's me, Smith," he said in a softer tone. "You know I love you and there is nothing you have to keep from me. If you need anything, ever, all you have to do is ask."

Smith knew he meant it. He did trust his uncle above anybody else. Well, except maybe Maylee.

Uncle Arnold bent his head and peered into Smith's face. "And," he encouraged with a smile, "I keep a dang good secret!"

Smith looked at the floor in silence for what seemed like a long time. Confusion, fear, and disappointment in himself all swirled through his head in a jumbled whirlwind of emotions. Why hadn't he thought to talk to Uncle Arnold? Now it sounded weird. He couldn't exactly say, *Hey, this guy got murdered so we thought we would investigate. We uncovered a conspiracy and we stole something from Qumran.* Or, could he? He finally glanced at his Uncle, regret in his eyes. "I was going to tell you but…" he began, his voice trailing off.

His uncle placed a strong hand on his knee. "It is never right to do the wrong thing," he began, "but doing the wrong thing and then hiding it is downright cowardly."

Smith's soft blue eyes welled with tears. If there was one thing he prided himself on, it was owning up when he had done something wrong. Now, he felt like he had let his uncle down and lost his respect.

Uncle Arnold placed a heavy arm around Smith's shoulders, and the boy turned his face and hid his tears in his uncle's shoulder. After a few minutes, the crying stopped and Uncle Arnold gave him a grim smile. "I think it's time to come clean," he said. Smith nodded, drew a deep breath, and started from the beginning.

Strangely, talking about the events not only lifted a great weight from Smith's shoulders, but also dissipated the cloud of confusion that had settled over what had actually happened. And, Uncle Arnold understood. He didn't judge them for sneaking out or even for starting their own investigation. But, he was worried about their safety.

"A man who has killed once has fewer qualms about killing again," he said. He looked sad, and he sounded like he knew what he was talking about. "I don't want that to be you or your sister or Rafi."

Smith nodded. He agreed wholeheartedly. He decided to tell his uncle what they discovered at Qumran. He reached under his pillow and unrolled the painting. "Look what we found hidden in one of the clay jars in a secret cave."

Uncle Arnold raised his eyebrows in question. "Secret cave?"

"Uh-huh," Smith answered. "Rafi got lost once and accidentally found it. So, we went back."

"And you found this in there?" he asked, tilting his head toward the painting.

"Ya, there was a group of people in there when we showed up. We heard them talking so we hid outside until they left. Thankfully, they went the other way. We hurried to search through the jars 'cause it sounded like they moved them to hide something. The tour group must have scared them because we heard them heading back. We bolted out the cave the way we came in."

Uncle Arnold was curious. Now he was taking this painting seriously. He leaned closer, scrutinizing the bumble bee caught in the moment of his day's work. "Why is the canvas that big for such a small painting?" he wondered aloud.

Smith just shook his head. "It's weird, right?" He hopped off the bed and reached for the sweatshirt he had thrown on the floor the night before. He had tucked the art case holding his souvenir inside, and wanted to show his uncle.

"What is really weird, is that they had put it in this case," he said, passing the case to his uncle. "The case is worth more than the art!"

"I see," Uncle Arnold mused thoughtfully. "Why not

either buy a junk case, or at least make the art plausible as being valuable if the idea is to trick someone. Is that what you're saying?"

"Exactly!" agreed Smith. "That art isn't going to fool anyone, so what's the point in having a quality case for it? I mean, I'm just a kid and I can tell it is garbage."

Uncle Arnold took a closer look at the case. It was a good quality, water-proof case that probably cost at least a hundred dollars.

He then turned his attention to the canvas Smith had handed him. Unrolling it, he spread it out on the floor, setting a shoe on each of its four corners to keep it flat. He noticed that it was slightly a different color around the edge where it must have been removed from its frame before being placed in the art case.

"Strange," he commented, "someone took some pains to remove this painting carefully. Many times, art thieves cut the canvas right out of its frame to save time. Either this person wasn't in a hurry, or didn't want to damage the canvas." Maybe it was the canvas itself that was valuable?

He flipped the painting over and stood peering at the under side of the canvas. It was slightly yellowed on the back side along its border, as if it had an accidental water mark of some kind. Uncle Arnold held it up, but the lighting in the room didn't allow him to make out any irregularities. Smith grinned at his uncle and hopped off the bed. "I have the perfect spot," he commented, leading his uncle to the closet. Inside, Smith turned on the glowing, uncovered light bulb with a bow and said, "ta-dah!"

Uncle Arnold grinned back at him and held the canvas

up, the painted side toward the light, peering at the blank side of the canvas. As the light peeked through the tiny holes of the canvas, a shadow formed on the side Uncle Arnold and Smith were looking at. Strangely enough, it was not the shape of the painted flower, but something much larger that took up the entire canvas except for the very outside edge.

Uncle and nephew looked at each other simultaneously. There was something inside!

Smith stood frozen to his spot in the closet, his huge grin baring all his teeth. A wiggle of excitement started in his big toe and worked its way up his entire body.

"Go, grab a knife," his uncle whispered. Smith raced to the kitchen. Seconds later, he returned and handed the knife to Uncle Arnold who said a quick prayer, then sliced a gash in the very top of the canvas where the glue and water had stained the cloth. The cut revealed that there was not simply one canvas, but two that had been meshed together to appear to be one piece. It was really a cleverly-crafted, giant envelope.

Uncle and nephew paused and looked at each other excitedly as time seemed to stop ticking. They both knew that they were about to uncover either the greatest disappointment of their lives, or the greatest religious discovery of the century.

Gingerly, Uncle Arnold lifted the skin of the canvas from the other side and peered in, the light from the closet casting a yellow glow onto his terse, white knuckles.

There, like royalty wrapped in beggar's clothes, The Queen lay tucked safely away in the shell of an ugly painting. "This document is thousands of years old," Uncle Arnold commented, half to himself. "The more rolling and unrolling we do, the more damage it causes. And, I don't want the oils from our skins depositing on the ancient manuscript," he said.

All of a sudden, the reality hit Smith and he paled. They had stolen The Queen from under the nose of a bunch of murderers. They were dead if anyone found out they had it!

"We have to take it somewhere safe!" Smith said, suddenly worried for the well-being of his friends and family. "They were planning to go back for it last night when the caves shut down. They know it's missing now!"

Uncle Arnold froze, and a chill ran down his spine. Smith was right. They couldn't keep this here. He snapped his fingers, a sign he had a solution. "C'mon!" he exclaimed, "I have an idea!"

Swiftly, he reached for his cell phone and dialed Amjad. "I need you to come for me in the car," he said urgently into the receiver. Amjad responded briefly, but Smith couldn't catch what he said. "Okay, see you shortly," Uncle Arnold said, ending the call.

"There is only one place where I trust to keep this scroll from getting into the wrong hands, and only one man for the job," Uncle Arnold said, looking at Smith with a mixture of excitement and worry. "I don't know if I should take you, it could be dangerous."

Smith twisted his face at his uncle. "Ya, right! I do all the thieving and the work, and you get all the fun and glory?" He shook his head. "No way! I'm going with you."

Uncle Arnold grunted his consent. Smith reminded him so much of himself, quiet and thoughtful, but brave and determined. Carefully, Uncle Arnold rolled the painting housing the scroll into a narrow tubular shape, and secured it in place with a hair tie of Maylee's that lay on the nightstand.

He looked around, searching for something to conceal the treasure in. The aluminum art case would be too obvious, he decided, but his eyes caught the gleam of Smith's wide mouth water bottle. He quickly took the lid off and made sure the inside was completely dry, wiping it thoroughly with his tee-shirt. Carefully, he placed the scroll inside and screwed the top on.

"That's ironic," Smith commented.

"What?" Uncle Arnold asked, tucking the water bottle under his arm.

"That's exactly what the Essenes did 2,000 years ago when they wanted to protect that very scroll. They placed it in a dish." He laughed and elbowed his uncle. "People don't change much."

It felt like they waited an eternity for Amjad. And every second mattered now. Finally, he beeped the horn and Smith and Arnold rushed from the house.

"Shrine of the Book, if you please, Driver," Uncle Arnold said with a laugh, "and proceed with the utmost caution. We are carrying precious cargo!"

EIGHTEEN

Back Underground

Abraham sat stunned at the old oak table covered in knots and decorated with small pots of different types of ink. The tip of his long, white beard just tickled the top of the table as he spoke.

"Good morning, Arnold. And Smith, you are back so soon! To what do I owe the honor of this visit?"

Arnold stepped forward. His demeanor spoke business. "Good morning, Rabbi," he said, extending his hand and handing the old man the metal bottle.

"What is this?" Abraham asked, taking it and unscrewing the top. He removed the painting and saw that it had been cut. He frowned at them, a reprimand on his tongue. Arnold interrupted him before he could start.

"Open it carefully," he said. "It's the inside that matters."

Abraham gently unbound the canvas and rolled it out on the long table. He placed a paperweight on each of the corners to keep the canvas from flipping back into a cylinder.

"This belonged to Kareem," Abraham said instantly, recognizing the painting. "It used to hang in his office."

He paused and drew a deep breath, eying Smith quizzically. Something told him this was related to their previous conversation about The Queen.

With heart fluttering but hands steady, he reached for a pair of delicate, metal pincers and slowly, carefully, grasped the edge of the hidden manuscript. It moved easily inside the canvas.

He closed his eyes, as if they were no good to him and began to see with his fingers, as though he could feel through the metal of the large tweezers. He paused and, moving his device to the left side, gently began easing the document out of its shell, inch by inch.

The scroll was fairly small in width, decently long, but broken into several pieces. Abraham extracted it and laid it gently on the old table, smoothing its worn edges with a delicate brush. Covering the delicate papyrus were the tiniest markings Smith had ever seen. There were no spaces, just rows and rows of perfectly shaped symbols packed tightly onto the manuscript like sardines in a can.

"Where on earth did you get this?"

"Err...I...uh..." Smith looked at his uncle for help. None came. "I found it," he said in a small voice.

Abraham's eyes were moist with tears of joy, but his mouth went dry as he tried to read the words. He swallowed hard, and slowly began again, reading aloud in his thick, Hebrew tongue. Uncle Arnold repeated after him, translating into English, "Now it came to pass in the days of Ahasuerus, (this is Ahasuerus which reigned, from India even unto Ethiopia, over an hundred and seven and twenty provinces:)..."

Abraham's voice cracked with emotion and he stopped reading. He turned and looked directly at Smith.

"Jehovah has seen fit to let my greatest desire be fulfilled in my lifetime on this earth. Know that you have brought an old man, an old scholar, the deepest joy possible. I praise Jehovah with my voice and my heart, and I thank you with the same."

He said all of this slowly and very sincerely, and raised his wrinkled hands to the sky as he spoke of Jehovah.

Smith was unsure what to say as he stared into the dark, intense eyes of the man—a Rabbi by calling, museum curator by profession. Smith simply smiled at him a sincere, knowing smile and looked at Uncle Arnold for help.

"Rabbi, we are entrusting it to you. I think the people that killed Benjamin know we have it.." Uncle Arnold's voice trailed off. He shook his head, an effort to clear it. He hated to bring his thoughts of the murderers into this quiet, lamp-lit room.

The Rabbi stood and placed a hand on Arnold's shoulder. "I will give my very life to protect it!"

Arnold nodded at him. Abraham was a good man.

"Let's roll," Arnold said quietly. They didn't want to stay any longer than necessary.

Abraham led them to the door, and his eyes glittered as he said, half in jest, "God, save the Queen!"

Smith and Uncle Arnold hurried down the halls and to the car while the Rabbi locked the door behind them. He sat down to work on the very tedious and delicate process of preserving the manuscript safely. He would protect it by cleaning it and making sure it was completely dry, then sealing it against the elements by covering it with an acid-free polyester coating and securing it between two pieces of fine glass. After it was stable, he would then begin to think about how and where to keep it hidden.

He hummed to himself softly as an idea floated to him. He smiled and praised Jehovah, thinking that indeed he made man very much like he made sheep—sweet, but fairly dumb. Both creatures tended to get themselves into delicate situations and then panic, trying everything except the logical solution. Abraham would play off of this defect in man and place the manuscript where no one would think to look—in the most obvious place of all!

* * *

Smith didn't say a word when they got back in the car. His mind was racing, a series of pictures flashing through his consciousness like a movie reel in slow motion. First, he saw old al-Rashad's hollow mouth laughing at them. Then the image snapped into the Garden of Gethsemane and Jack lazily leaning on the wall while Ben's body grew cold just out of sight. He saw Abraham in his study and how his face darkened at the mention of Johann Barker's name.

The problem was, Smith had no idea how to put this information together. Now the Queen was supposedly safe with Abraham, but what if Big Dale and his crew found it again? What would they do to the old Rabbi? And, how did they find it in the first place?

The only fact that consoled Smith at all was that he had Uncle Arnold on his side. His confidant and protector had come through after all.

Back at the house, Smith slipped inside to call an emergency meeting with Maylee and Rafi. On the way in, he heard Amjad's quiet voice strained with urgency. He could only make out one word, but it was enough to shake his newly found confidence. *Followed.*

NINETEEN

Suspicions About Amjad

Maylee crawled across the balcony and onto Rafi's side of the wall. She hadn't waited for an invitation. As a matter of fact, it hadn't even occurred to her. Smith had disappeared with the painting and hadn't returned, and she needed to get to Rafi.

She found him standing quietly on a mat, his palms out, silently partaking in *salah*, ritual prayer. She forgot her urgency as she watched the art and beauty in his religious moment. His prayer was like a dance. He moved so gracefully, standing first, then bending. Eventually he was completely prostrate, his forehead to the ground. He sat back on his heels to finish, his movements corresponding with the segment of prayer to his Allah.

Rafi felt her watching him, but refused to let her presence break his concentration. During prayer, all his thoughts should be on Allah. To think about anything else was to have an adulterated mind. It took concentration to really commune with the Most High. After he finished *salah*, he turned his full attention to her. He noticed she came alone.

She looked at him shyly as he sauntered over to the grapefruit tree. She was frozen there, unable to move or stop staring at Rafi as he came closer. He climbed partway up the tree, stopping a few feet underneath her.

He knew he was making her more uncomfortable with every step. He liked that he could make her feel that way. "Good morning," he said.

"Hi," Maylee managed to squeak.

"Come on," Rafi urged, grabbing her hand and nearly pulling her out of the tree. "Where is Smith?"

They sat down in the shade, their backs rested against the trunk of the tree. "I don't know. That's what I came to tell you. I went with my mom and aunt to pick up a few groceries and when I came back, he was gone." She looked at him intently with huge gray eyes. "So is the painting."

Rafi looked at her seriously. "You don't know where he went?"

Maylee shook her head and looked down at her hands. She picked a piece of grass and stared at it for a long time.

Rafi could sense her worry for her brother. He put his arm around her shoulders and felt her stiffen before she softened into his embrace. "He will be okay," Rafi whispered, brushing her hair back from her forehead with his hand.

Maylee felt safe with her head on Rafi's shoulder. She turned to look at him as he spoke. The corners of his mouth edged up slightly in a smile and he ran his finger along her cheek. She smiled back at him and didn't move as he leaned in to kiss the tip of her nose. She giggled as he drew back from her. He leaned in again, slowly this time, kissing her nose, her eyes, and finally pausing before her lips.

Her heart was beating so fast. He made her feel different. So alive. So nervous. Her stomach balled into a knot and she could hardly breathe. She could feel his warm breath on her skin and she couldn't pull her gaze away from his eyes. She had just decided to kiss him back when she heard a scrambling in the tree above them. She sat up and scooted away quickly, just as Smith dropped to the ground in front of them.

Maylee had never seen her brother looking so wild before. The usually calm Smith stood in front of them, out of breath and trembling.

"It really was The Queen!" he blurted, grasping a tree branch over his head to support himself. "We took a knife and cut it and gave it to Abraham. It is broken into pieces but it's all there."

"Whoa, whoa, whoa! Slow down and start over, please." Maylee held her hand up in a *stop!* gesture as she spoke.

Smith breathed deeply. He was still standing. He started pacing and counting on his fingers as he spoke. "Okay. This morning, Uncle Arnold came in to wake me up. Oh, yeah," he directed at Maylee, "we are in trouble by the way."

"Why?"

"Ditching Amjad."

Maylee shrugged her shoulders.

"Anyways…" she guided her brother.

"Well, I ended up telling him what happened in the Garden of Gethsemane and at Qumran."

"Smith!" Maylee and Rafi said at the same time.

"I know, I know. The less people involved, the better. But, we can trust Uncle Arnold. He actually helped me find out the secret of the painting."

"Which is what we have been trying to get to this whole

time. Get to the point, Smith!" Maylee said, annoyed.

"You know how the painting was too small for the canvas? Like someone had only painted the center and forgot the rest?"

Rafi and Maylee nodded.

"Well, Uncle Arnold thought that was weird too. Plus, the carrying case it was in wasn't cheap. Things just weren't stacking up. Uncle Arnold took a closer look, and when you hold it up to the light, you can see that there is really something inside of the painting. Like when you hold up an envelope and can see the letter inside."

"Wow!" Maylee interjected. "So how do you really know it is The Queen."

"We cut the canvas with a knife and found the scroll inside. Uncle Arnold didn't want to touch the scroll itself or try to remove it, so we took it to Abraham at the Shrine of the Book. He promised to keep it safe. He's working on preserving it right now."

Rafi ran his fingers through his curly hair. He spoke for the first time, visibly upset. "That makes things really dangerous for Abraham." The old man was almost a father to him.

"But you should have seen him when he discovered the scroll," Smith countered. "He was so happy. He thanked me. Said it was his whole life's work."

"Oh, no doubt that is the best place for it," inserted Rafi. "But, I'm still worried about the Rabbi's safety."

"Ya," Smith agreed, "his and ours both."

"How would anyone know that we were even involved with the scroll?" Maylee asked.

"I have no clue how, but I heard Amjad tell Uncle Arnold we were followed."

"Wait, Amjad is in on this too?" Rafi asked, anger rising to boil in his eyes.

"I don't know if Amjad knows. Uncle Arnold just called him and told him we needed to get to the Israel Museum ASAP."

Rafi sadly shook his head. "If Amjad knows, this could get ugly really fast. I don't trust him at all. The streets have eyes, the walls have ears, and everyone has a price. Big Dale and the others who are out to get this scroll will stop at nothing. We have seen the evidence of that," Rafi said, referring to Benjamin Flickermann. It felt more like a lifetime than just a few days since the murder.

"Here's the thing," Rafi began. "We really can't rule out anyone.

"You know," inserted Maylee, "I almost wonder if Uncle Arnold has had someone watching us. How else would he know to confront Smith?"

Smith glared at her. Notes of a challenge hung in his tone. "Why would he spy on his own niece and nephew?"

Maylee shrugged her shoulders. "I don't know. The same reason he makes us go everywhere with Amjad? Maybe he just wants us to be safe. Or maybe he has actually known about the scroll for a long time." She leaned forward, closer to Smith, her cold eyes boring into his. "Maybe he knew all along and just convinced you to help him figure out the piece of the puzzle he couldn't quite solve."

"He's a good man!" Smith said loudly. Too loud. He lowered his voice to almost a whisper. "He's not like our deadbeat dad!"

Maylee seethed at him. She held his angry gaze with her own. "*Your* deadbeat dad," she hissed. "I stopped having a father the moment he walked out on all of us."

They couldn't look at each other. It just hurt too much. The very memories they clung too were the same memories they so desperately wanted to forget. And the truth always comes out under pressure.

Maylee picked up her blade of grass again and concentrated on it, letting it ground her. When she spoke again, the storm in her eyes had calmed. "Everyone has their price," she said slowly, quoting Rafi's words back to the group in a tense echo. "Say he did have someone following us for all the right reasons and that person sold us out to the bad guys, telling them that we had seen what happened in the Garden?"

The three friends looked at each other tensely as the same thought came to all of them at the same time. Maylee was the first to voice what they were all thinking. "Amjad!"

"But it was still pure chance that we found the scroll at the Dead Sea the following day," Smith commented. "They would have no idea that we were going to be there."

"Amjad is up in your family's business like ants on honey. Guaranteed he knew we were going to Qumran. Put that together with them knowing we were at the Garden and bam! The whole picture comes together," Rafi explained.

"Think about it," Maylee inserted. She started counting on her fingers. "Amjad was with us when we went to old al-Rashad. He took us to the Israel Museum. He probably knew about Qumran. Granted he wasn't involved in any of our conversations at Mahane Yehuda or at the Shrine of the Book, but if he knew about the Garden he could put the rest together."

"It still doesn't explain why the Queen was back at Qumran the very day we went," Smith said. The idea really bothered him. Rafi and Maylee didn't care as much, so Smith kept his thoughts to himself. *Whoever hid the scroll at Qumran that day did it because they had no other option. Something scared them. But what?*

His thoughts landed on something tangible and stopped. "Wait a second," Smith continued, turning pale. "The man who said goodbye to us after the tour, he didn't have an Israeli accent, remember? He could have been the same person who met up with the Americans in the Garden. We didn't get a good look at his face because he never came completely out of the dark, but it would fit that he could be the same person!"

"So maybe Amjad told them we had been at the Garden of Gethsemane and then warned them that we were in Qumran that day. Maybe they had other plans for the scroll and then decided to hide it and go back for it later when they found out we were there," Maylee added.

Rafi sighed, exhausted with the possibilities. "Too many what ifs, too many maybes," he said. "The problem is, we don't actually know anything."

"There is only one way to find out," Smith said definitively. "We know that they are going to be meeting again in the Garden. When they get there, we will be waiting for them!"

Rafi looked into the eyes of his friends. Both of them looked worried, scared, and yet very determined.

"If we tell Uncle Arnold, there is no way he will let us go," Maylee stated factually. "And, if he has someone follow us and that person is compromised by the enemy, we won't make it out alive."

Rafi sighed. "You're right," he agreed. "The less people who know about this, the better. We have to plan a way to leave a clue that only Mr. Arnold will understand, in case we don't make it back. But we also have to find a way to escape the eyes of anyone he might have watching us."

"Well," Maylee said matter-of-factly, "it's Tuesday. The rendezvous is tomorrow night. We better figure it out quick!"

TWENTY

A Sacrifice

Abraham sat, and with painstaking care, he smoothed the scroll, dusting it with his delicate brush. He read the words lovingly as the reality of the situation slowly settled in with him. He imagined another scribe, another scholar thousands of years before his time seated at a table much like this one. He too would have worn the *tefillin*, the sacred writings bound about his arm and his head in order to keep the Word of God on his mind and his heart.

Just as he did every time he inspected an ancient manuscript, Abraham admired the skill and the precision of the scribes who dedicated their lives to preserving Jehovah's commandments. There was no room for error here, no eraser, no white out, no delete button. Entire books were copied on one piece of parchment, papyrus, or animal skin, perfect down to every jot and tittle. For these men, it was more than a job; it was a passion, a love for history and an awe and respect for the sacred.

Abraham worked tirelessly preparing the piece for its preservation. The scroll was cracked in several places where it had been folded and where the papyrus had become brittle. He took care with the fragments, laying them carefully in order so as not to disrupt the meaning of the story as it flowed.

Finally, when he was satisfied, he rose up on his creaking legs and shuffled to a tall cupboard that stood in a corner. He took out two matching pieces of glass and gently set the flattened scroll inside, like a picture in a frame. He sealed the pieces together with small metal clamps, and grasped the masterpiece in his hands.

He walked back to the cupboard and reaching around the back, found the hidden lever. The cupboard sprung forward silently, revealing a dimly lit secret passage, knowledge that few were privy to. Turning, he slid behind the cupboard and closed the secret entrance behind him.

Abraham found himself in a narrow passage that ran underground between the museum itself and the Shrine of the Book, working his way towards the inner holding rooms of the museum where the items that weren't on display were safely stored. In the storage rooms, he walked by a Rembrandt painting, a sculpture by Michelangelo, and a treasure trove of ancient Egyptian bangles that shone with the dull luster of pure gold. Various ancient manuscripts lay stacked, glass to glass in an airtight carton, much like posters are arranged for previewing in a store.

Abraham opened the container housing the manuscripts. It hissed at him as he released the lever. Carefully, he sifted through the documents, counting as he went. Three… four…five…six. He paused at the seventh. The label read Instructions for embalming cats—Egypt. He slid the Queen into the seventh slot, grinning to himself as he imagined Jehovah would approve. He took the embalming document and decided to display it in the museum among some of the other ancient Egyptian writings, a change so slight in the large museum, only he would notice.

Abraham smiled to himself as he calmly strolled back through the hidden halls of the museum building that was in the compound. Once again, one of the ancient Bible texts was safe in the belly of the earth, hidden from the hands of power-hungry men. He silently entered his private alcove, appearing from behind the cabinet like a ghost.

Walking amongst the centuries of history had cleared his head as it tended to do. The realization that his lifetime was merely a breath on a cold morning that would disappear almost instantly helped his perspective. He would serve Jehovah without fear. He had prayed for wisdom, now he had to act like he had it.

There was only one solution. Only one way to keep The Queen safe. Abraham didn't like it one tiny bit. Sometimes there just isn't a right answer. Abraham reached for his phone, and forsaking his pride, dialed a number he knew by heart.

It rang three times. Four. Abraham thought maybe he wouldn't answer. Finally, on the sixth ring, a quiet voice spoke into the receiver. "Abraham," the voice said. "It's been a long time."

"It has, Johann."

"It must be important for you to call."

Abraham swallowed hard. He hated asking favors in general. But he especially didn't want to ask one of Johann Barker. "It is of utmost importance," he said gravely.

"Go on."

"I need a favor. Something risky, to protect an old friend."

Silence blared across the receiver. Johann finally spoke. "An old friend?"

"Yes, and the most lovely lady I have ever seen. The other love of our lives that we shared." A note of bitterness tinged his voice.

Abraham could hear Johann catch his breath on the other side. He knew.

"And, how can I help?"

"I'm afraid that is the hard part. She needs a twin. You are the only one with a blank papyrus that fits the time frame." Abraham closed his eyes and winced. There. He said it.

Johann spoke without hesitation. "It's yours. I'll bring it myself. Long live the Queen."

The phone clicked in Abraham's ear. "Yes, long live the Queen," he echoed to no one.

The plan had been set. The old Rabbi closed his eyes and extended his hands towards the Heavens. He prayed fervently for his faithful friend, Arnold, and he prayed for forgiveness for the plan that brought him so much guilt, yet would preserve the sanctity of the Word of God.

Ranya knocked briefly on Abraham's office door before popping her head in around 5:30. It was a Tuesday, so the museum didn't close until 10:00 that night.

"Johann Barker came by," she said, trying to keep the question out of her voice. Everyone knew Johann and Abraham didn't communicate. "He left a package for you, said it's urgent."

Abraham nodded, standing up from his table and walking toward her. She handed him a flat, lightweight package, huge question marks in her eyes.

"Thank you," he said, dismissing her. A hand-written note accompanied the delivery. *Let's get this over with,* he thought. The note was, of course, from Johann.

Abraham,

I must admit that it was your example that prompted me to also sacrifice something I hold dear for the sake of the greater good. I know that my sacrifice can never pay for what you have lost, but I assure you that my heart breaks all day, every day, year after year for Alice as well. I know neither of us will ever forget or forgive; some things are far too painful.

One word of warning as you proceed: Jerome Hassan should not be trusted. I have reason to believe he was highly involved in the death of Benjamin Flickermann and that he also was in possession of The Queen before she found sanctuary with you.

May the Lord guide you and protect you.

Johann

Abraham folded the note and setting it down, turned his attention to the package. Willing his hands steady, he opened it. There it was. He just stared at it for a while. A papyrus manuscript, wilted and cracked, passable as one of the Dead Sea Scrolls. Except for one thing. It was completely blank. No writing, no markings, and no invisible ink they could draw out. Sighing he got up from the table to brew a pot of coffee. It was going to be a long night of painstaking work.

TWENTY-ONE

Monster Park

C arol and Adah sat on a blanket of grass under a shady tree in the *Mifletzet*, the Monster Park. Carol watched as her kids followed Rafi into a giant monstrosity. It was a huge, melting cow with three red tongues that served as slides. Rafi was the first to step into the Monster's throat and climb the dark stairway the Monster had swallowed.

It was hot and stuffy inside. Maylee could hear the echo of voices in different languages bouncing off the walls. The screams were all the same, though, as the kids from all over the world yelped happily as they slid off the hot, red tongues.

They were thankful for one thing in particular today. Amjad wasn't with them. They all relaxed just a little bit and were actually enjoying climbing all over the Monster.

Two girls just a little younger than Smith were eying him from identical faces. They were twins from Britain, he discovered. He was infatuated with the way they talked, saying words he could understand in an accent that was too cute to be true. Maylee decided they were evil. Playing with her brother like the Siamese cats played with the goldfish in Lady and the Tramp.

"I'll wager you can't beat us from the top," one of the little twins challenged.

"I suppose he's a chicken liver," the other sighed, looking sadly at her sister.

"Bet!" Smith called out as he raced through the throat of
the monster and to the top of the slide.

Maylee rolled her eyes. Smith was so dumb to fall for
their little game. The twins sat on either side of him on the
other two tongues.

"One," Smith counted. "Two…" He didn't have a chance
to say "three" because the twins decided to go on the count
of two and leave him behind.

"He's really slow on the slide," one little voice whispered
to the other, just loud enough for Smith to hear.

"Hey, not fair!" he argued. "You went on two. You have
to wait to three."

The twins exchanged a knowing glance. "Well, if it
would make him feel better, we could race again."

Rafi and Maylee followed them into the throat. Rafi
stopped Maylee as she was about to scramble up the stairs.
He grabbed her by her arms and twirled her around so that
he was in front of her.

A laugh danced in his eyes. "Beat you!" he taunted.

"Nuh-uh!" Maylee countered. "You cheated!"

She tried to wriggle past him on the stairs, but both of
his arms were blocking her. She tried to duck underneath
one, but he was too quick. He started to scramble his way up
the stairs in front of her, but she grabbed his arm. She might
not get past him, but he wasn't going to beat her without a
fight.

He had her right where he wanted her. She was cling-
ing to one arm and he wrapped his other arm around her.

Suddenly, they were very close. She stopped laughing and struggling and stood very still on the stairs, breathing hard. Neither of them had winning on their minds anymore.

Maylee was nervous. He had taken her by surprise and all of a sudden, she didn't hear any screams coming from Monster Park, only the sound of her own heart beating.

"I, uh…" She licked her lips and swallowed, trying to keep her voice from cracking in her dry throat. "I wonder if Smith…" She couldn't make a solid sentence.

Rafi saved her the trouble. Leaning down, he brushed his lips against hers softly. He tasted like honey and his warm breath escaped from his nose and tickled her cheek. She could see him smile in the darkness. He turned and headed up the stairs and down the slide.

She stood still for a moment, cemented to that stair. Smith and the twins rushed by her, and she slowly climbed behind them. This time when she went down the slide, she didn't scream. All of her senses were overpowered with the feel of Rafi's lips as they briefly touched hers.

Maylee went up and down the slide like a zombie. She lost track of how many times. She kept trying to avoid getting caught alone with Rafi on the stairs, and yet, secretly hoping it would happen again. *I could learn a thing or two from those British twins*, she thought, annoyed with herself. The feeling with Rafi was so strong it paralyzed her. *Why didn't I just kiss him back?*

Next thing she knew, Smith had grabbed her arm and was dragging her up the steps and pointing across the park. Smith had forgotten about the blond twins from England and what he showed her made Maylee forget about her moment with Rafi.

She saw him. Dark sunglasses hid his eyes, but she recognized him anyway. The way he sat so rigidly, nervously picking at his fingernails. Every now and again, he would jerk his head up and glance around him. Then back to picking.

"Ugh!" she said in disgust. "Amjad." The thought of him watching them all the time made her itch.

Smith turned pale. They were hunted, trapped like a bug in a spider's web. Amjad was slowly spinning them up with his web into a tightly managed cocoon until they couldn't escape. How did he always know where they would be?

"Tell Rafi," he whispered.

Maylee nodded at him and stepped back into the warped throat. *One step at a time,* she thought as she forced herself to breathe. *In and out. In and out.* They had to think clearly to get away from him.

Rafi saw her and grinned, but his playful smile disappeared when he saw her expression.

"He's here," she said urgently.

"Amjad?"

She nodded.

He said a phrase she didn't understand in Arabic, but it sounded bad. "C'mon. We need to get out of here."

They exited and found Smith between his mom and aunt. He was complaining of a stomachache and threatening to throw up. Maylee just shook her head in awe. *Man, is he good!* she thought. The women immediately began packing their things up. Adah flagged down a taxi driver just as he was dropping off a fresh load of tourists at the *Mifletzet.*

Rafi glanced around. Amjad was nowhere in sight.

Gone. Poof. Just like that. The real monster was nowhere to be seen in Monster Park. Rafi was the last to hop into the cab. He got in slowly, deliberately, eying his surroundings. Finally he slammed the door and the car whirred away.

No one paid attention to the old man reading a newspaper and sipping a Coke. If they had, they probably wouldn't have recognized him as the same man who had bumped them on the bus to the Dead Sea when Smith had slipped and mentioned the Queen.

As they left, he put up his newspaper. No need to fake reading it anymore. He also snatched a cab. *No rush, Driver,* he thought. A part of him wanted to yell, "Follow that taxi!" but it really wasn't necessary. He just gave the driver Arnold Kempler's address instead.

*   *   *

Back at the house, they held an emergency meeting under Rafi's grapefruit tree.

"I say we spy on Amjad," Maylee stated. "Right now, he has the upper hand because he is always watching us. We can reverse that on him."

"I don't get it," Smith said.

"Clearly they know exactly where we go and when. If we watch Amjad, we can figure out how to get past him. Especially since he doesn't know we are on to him."

"That just might work," Rafi said. It had to work. The meeting in the Garden was happening in just eight hours.

"How do you propose we do this spying?" Smith asked.

"I'll stay in this tree and watch. You guys should go to bed like normal, but be prepared to head out when I give the signal," Rafi suggested.

"You don't really know what you are looking for though," Smith interjected.

"Trust me, if anything is less than normal in this neighborhood, I will be able to put my finger on it. I will figure out where he is watching from and then we will get out of here and to the Garden in a way he won't see us."

"This is it, guys," Maylee said softly. They all understood how serious this was. The boys nodded at her. Smith climbed the tree back to their balcony. Maylee was following behind him but Rafi caught her hand briefly. She smiled at him sweetly. He just stared at her intently.

"It's gonna be okay," he promised.

She nodded and turning, proceeded up the tree and over the wall.

* * *

Really annoying, that's what this is, Amjad thought as he slapped at a mosquito that buzzed in his ear. *Here I am, creeping through Monster Park like a pedophile to keep an eye on these kids!*

Being Mr. Kempler's right hand man had been a great job. Until his family came to town to visit. Suddenly, he wasn't focused on uniting Muslims and Jews any more or even watching hockey film and planning new strategies for Peace Players International. Instead, he was tromping down the hot streets in his dress slacks making sure these little twits didn't get into trouble.

He sat down trying to look nonchalant when he noticed Adah and Carol a few yards away from him on the grass. *I need a new spot,* he thought as he stood up and took a steady pace for the trees.

As he reached to dust off his pants, he felt something stuck to the material behind his right knee. He turned awkwardly to inspect it. A lime green gumball had been thoroughly chewed until there was no flavor and then spewed out in rejection. Thanks to his lack of luck, he just happened to sit at the very spot it landed. *I don't get paid enough for this!* he thought, his blood boiling.

He was a man better suited to air-conditioned offices and business meetings, leather-coated chairs and iced coconut water. Trailing kids through parks and shuffling down alleyways just wasn't his thing.

He made his way through the trees, combing his way through several spider webs just in time to see the five of them load into a taxi. His eyes narrowed as he watched Rafi take a long look around the park before he entered the vehicle. *You think you're something else, don't you little boy? We will see about that!*

An idea came to him as he watched the taxi pull away. Necessity is indeed the mother of invention, and he needed to be out of this cat-and-mouse game. Or, at least be winning.

He smiled to himself. He had all the supplies he needed at his home. Except for extra batteries. He whistled as he walked to Arnold's car and hopped in, cranking up the air conditioner. He sat there for a moment, enjoying the cool air and the dull hum of the engine.

He looked at the clock on the radio. 11:53 a.m. Plenty of time. He sped off, joining the whir of traffic. He made a mental calculation. Get batteries from the store, head home, *Project Follow* will be in progress by 12:25. The thought made him smile. Maybe he would even have time for a light lunch.

TWENTY-TWO

A Threat

Arnold sat at his desk, cradling his head in his hands. He hated dealing with situations like this. He caught a glimpse of himself in the glass door. Little tufts of hair were out of place, reflecting the tension that sailed through the office and on to the ice.

He picked up his hockey magazine and thumbed through it without really seeing it. Instead, he was hearing the same conversation replay over and over in his mind.

Yesterday. It had happened on the ice. The only place in Jerusalem where these things didn't have to take place. The rink was a neutral territory for these boys. They left their religious and cultural differences at the door and put on a jersey that unified them. Well, that was how it was supposed to happen.

Arnold knew it was going to be ugly as soon as he saw Efran and Jerod force Kinza against the wall of the rink. Arnold was a swift skater, and this was the time to use that skill. The sharp blades of his skates spit ice shavings onto the Jewish brothers as he slid to a halt in front of them.

Efran and Jerod looked at him coldly, testosterone hardening their eyes. Efran gripped his hockey stick horizontally across Kinza's throat, pinning him against the edge of the rink. He didn't look willing to let go, either.

Arnold towered over the teenage boys. He looked them flatly in the eyes for several seconds before he said a single word. "Enough," he said quietly, but with an authority that could punch through a two-by-four.

Without breaking his gaze, Efran released his Muslim teammate and split the hockey stick over his knee, thrusting the pieces at Kinza.

"Be glad I broke that stick and not you," he threatened as he turned to speed across the ice. Jerod called Kinza a name under his breath before he followed his brother.

In defiance, Kinza spat onto the ice trail they left. The team was split now. The Muslims lingered on one side of the rink, the Jews on the other. Kinza skated to his side with his Muslim brothers. Everyone stared at the centre line, daring anyone to cross that boundary.

Arnold skated up and placed one foot on either side of the line. "Bring it in," he commanded. Practice was over for the day. The boys reluctantly obeyed, still refusing to cross the centre line.

It didn't matter who had started it. The fact it was happening at practice was a problem. Arnold couldn't understand it. At the same time, he knew what he had signed up for when he took on the challenge of running an interracial team. He was a Messianic Jew who had married an Arab woman. He thought he had the necessary experience to weld these boys together, to create a team that crossed the divide that had driven the cousins apart for centuries. Normally, he was quite successful. Yesterday, he felt he had failed.

He was putting the magazine down and turning to the hated task of calling parents on both sides of the conflict when something slipped from between the pages. An index card brushed the table, landing on the floor face down. Black ink had seeped to the surface like an ugly bruise. Arnold picked it up without a second thought and flipped it over.

WHAT YOU VALUE MOST IS IN DANGER. WHAT WILL YOU BE WILLING TO TRADE FOR IT? SHRINE OF THE BOOK, TONIGHT 10:00 P.M.

He sat stunned for a moment. He had been expecting a magazine renewal card, not a threat and it threw him off guard. Maybe it wasn't for him? A joke? Something the mail carrier had accidentally shoved in his pile of mail?

Arnold swept a hand through his hair as the realization struck him. This was about the scroll. Amjad said they had been followed, but how? And why? He had barely discovered that his niece and nephew had confiscated the scroll from Qumran when he and Smith rushed it to Abraham.

He had no choice. To the Shrine of the Book he would go. Whoever wrote the note knew they had left him no option. But as to what he would do when he got there, well, he didn't have a plan yet. And he was a man who liked to have a plan. He prayed to God for the wisdom to handle the situation well, and picking up the phone, continued business as usual.

The hours took their sweet time until finally, the Muslim call to prayer rang throughout the city. He was glad that it was midday, and anxious at the same time. *Tick, tock. Tick, tock.* Decision time was creeping up on him. He decided to call his wife. He wanted to hear the voice he loved so much before it was so powerful it could keep him from the museum. He knew very well it could be the last time.

"Hello, I'm looking for a Mrs. Adah Jones," he said playfully into the receiver. Adah laughed back at him.

"I love you," she said with a smile, instantly recognizing his voice.

"I won't be home until late tonight," he said sadly.

He could almost hear her pouting.

"Everything okay, babe?"

He swallowed hard as he prepared to lie to his wife. "Ya, things are fine. Problems with the boys won't be resolved over the phone. I'm having Amjad drive me to their houses to speak in person. You know how these things go. Don't wait up, okay?"

A little of the light that typically shone from Adah's eyes faded as she ached for her husband. He had so much to deal with, the pressures of not only running a team of teenage boys, but all of the internal problems that gnawed at the intestines of Israel.

She took the bait, and he knew it. He didn't tell her about the note. Adah wasn't the type of woman to sit back and cry. She would do something. Which is one of the reasons he married her in the first place. But not this time. He wanted her home safe with the kids and his sister. Some things, a man just has to do alone.

Arnold sat at his desk and stared for a long time at two pictures. One was of him and Adah two summers prior on a sailboat, smiling carefree at the camera. The other was a Christmas greeting card that Carol had sent of their family in the States. He kissed the photos and reaching for his coat, he headed for the door.

He had six hours before he had to make his way to the museum. He planned on eating a big dinner and even drinking a soda. A Coke, probably. Something he rarely did. It might be his last meal for a while. He snatched his laptop and tucked it safely in his briefcase. He was also going to do some research on the scroll, see if he could find how he and his family were linked to all of this.

He pulled out his cell phone to call Amjad for a ride, then thought twice. He opted for a taxi this time.

"Ten minutes," the operator said. Perfect. Next, he dialed Amjad.

He answered on the second ring, as usual. The young man was always available. One of the reasons Arnold loved working with him, actually.

"Amjad," He greeted him. "You busy?"

"Not at all," Amjad lied, putting away his tools. He was always taking apart machines and modifying them as he rebuilt them. Sometimes, he even had to create his own tools before he could really carry out the plan he envisioned. Right then, he happened to be adding a turbocharger to a gasoline powered remote-control monster truck, fully equipped with a video cam that was linked to display to his laptop. He had Rafi and his little friends in mind with this one.

"Great," responded Arnold. "Look, uh…" he took a deep breath before he could continue. "I need you to keep an eye on Adah and the kids for me. I won't be going home until late tonight."

No response from the other end of the line.

Arnold felt the need to explain given Amjad's silence. "I know it is a lot to ask of you. God knows I wish I wasn't in this position!" He paused, raking his fingers through his hair. His voice was shaky when he finally spoke again. "Just keep them safe, okay? Promise me, no matter what, you will make sure they are okay?"

"I will do everything I can to help your family," Amjad promised quietly.

Arnold breathed a sigh of relief. "Until we meet again, my friend," Arnold bade him goodbye. "*Allah Ma-ak*," Amjad said in return. God be with you.

Arnold watched from behind glass doors as the taxi screeched to halt outside the hockey complex. *This car could handle some new brakes,* he thought as he exited into the heat.

A red-faced driver greeted him and asked his destination. Arnold could feel the sweat beading up behind his collar and on his cheeks. Four windows rolled down was a clear sign that the air conditioning in the car was also due to be replaced.

"Grand Café, please," he instructed. The Open Toast from Paris sandwich they served would be just right. If his nerves would allow him to keep it down. As the sweat drops grew larger and began trickling over his skin, he thought a cold bottle of water wouldn't hurt either. And, Grand Café had an interesting and diverse clientele. Between that and Google, he was hoping to find some answers before he headed to the Shrine of the Book that night.

TWENTY-THREE

Suspicions

A long wooden bar lined the wall of the Grand Café. A few tables sprinkled here and there completed the seating arrangements. It had a homey feel that allowed the customers to relax and talk freely over a cup of coffee or a bite to eat.

Uncle Arnold found a spot up at the bar. He glanced around the coffee shop and quickly summed up the other four guests.

Perched in a seat next to the window was a dark-skinned Arab. The gray beret he wore framed warm, chocolate eyes that blinked more than average. He wore a light linen shirt that covered his arms all the way to his wrists, covered by a black zip-up vest.

About ten feet deeper into Grand Café sat an unlikely couple. A small Asian woman in a lavender tee-shirt kept laughing. She couldn't keep her conversation alive without flailing her tiny arms to punctuate every sentence. The man who sat across from her merely grunted. Maybe they didn't speak the same language? He was a tall, coolly dressed European with wire-rimmed glasses so thin a sneeze could have left him frameless. *Not to worry,* Arnold thought, *he looks like a man incapable of sneezing.*

That left one other person. Now, to the good part, he thought. He had actually noticed the man as soon as he walked in the door and had sidled up as close as possible without looking obvious.

Maybe it was the mismatched shoes that had drawn his attention. Possibly the fact the man had eaten the center out of his pastry and held it up to his face, blinking through the hole suspiciously at Arnold as he interrupted the scene. Helpful or not, the conversation he was about to initiate at least promised to be interesting.

First off, Arnold decided to pick up the man's tab. He was so thin! *Probably one of the many homeless that line the streets,* he thought sadly. It was the least he could do for the man who was struggling to gum his pastry into a mush before swallowing it.

A brief moment of guilt hit Arnold as he thought of the sandwich he had ordered from the server. How he was planning to make the most of his mouth full of teeth and devour it. The guilt left as his sandwich arrived and his stomach rumbled.

Ttsss. He cracked open his can of Coke. That got the old man's attention. His eyes focused and he zoomed in on Arnold's table like a shark that smells blood. Arnold was amazed. One little sound and he was in. He motioned to the server.

"Make it two," he said, raising the soda.

The server nodded and reached into a cooler.

"For my friend here," Arnold said, motioning with his head toward the old man.

Flaps of extra skin rippled as the old man smiled a huge

toothless grin and began clapping wildly. A throaty chuckle crawled from his mouth as the server set the can in front of him on the bar counter.

He grasped the can in both of his hands and kissed it profusely. Droplets of condensation formed on the outside of the aluminum as it contacted the warmer air. A gleam played in his eyes as he stuck out his tongue and lapped up one of the drops. Then another. Then another.

Until that moment, Arnold had never seen the benefit of not having any teeth. The man had almost twice as much room in his mouth as the average person with a full set. It gave the illusion that his jaws actually opened wider, kind of like a snake's jaw that unhinges. For a moment, Arnold thought he was going to forget to open the can and swallow the soda whole.

The old man stuck out his bottom lip in a pout. All the condensation was gone. He sighed, and decided to fumble with the top. All of his fingernails were extremely long, disgustingly so, except for the pinky on his left hand. He must have broken that one. He desperately tried to slide that little pinky under the tab and pop it up, but the coordination just wasn't there. He scratched his scabby head that boasted at least ten spurting hairs, covering his stool with a fresh blanket of dead skin.

"Allow me," Arnold offered, reaching for the can. He made a mental note to hit the bathroom and wash his hands before he resumed his lunch.

The man eyed him suspiciously and clung to the can, covering it with his spindly arms. He glared at him from jaundiced eyes and whispered one word. "Mine!"

Arnold picked up his own can. He moved the tab back and forth. "I'll help you open it."

The old man was tempted. He plucked at the tab with his crusty fingernails, but it continued to snap back at him without piercing the aluminum. He let out a resigned sigh and handed it to Arnold, refusing to look at him as he opened it with ease.

He set it down on the bar in front of him and the old man was giddy again. He carefully took a tiny sip, leaping down from his stool and clapping to celebrate. It was so good, so refreshing, so out-of-this-world.

To the old man, the pact was set. Life was all about trades. "Ask me!" he commanded in a powerful voice that took Arnold by surprise.

The man had climbed back onto the stool and crossing his scrawny legs, perched his elbows on the table, his chin resting in the upward palms of his hands. He was waiting.

The server piped in. "You should," he suggested. "He knows all the gossip worth knowing in Jerusalem before it even happens."

The old man laughed heartily, grasping his belly with his hands. When the laughter subsided, he shook a gnarled finger at the server as if to say *Good joke!*

Here is my chance, Arnold thought. *After all, there is always Google if this doesn't pan out.* He asked, and the old man answered.

For the next fifteen minutes, old al-Rashad proceeded to tell Arnold all about Kareem Hassan and his fortune, his greedy sons, and the grandsons he left penniless. For the wealth of information he gave him, Arnold thought that soda must be high on al-Rashad's value scale.

* * *

It was getting late when Rafi finally noticed something out of the norm. Even though the sun had set an hour before, it was just beginning to get truly dark and the shadows were beginning to morph into inky blackness. It was that time of night where shapes were difficult to distinguish and where animals could slink through the shadows unnoticed by predators.

Of course! Rafi admitted as he watched a dark sedan slither along the street, easing to a stop three houses away from him. The car was nicely camouflaged from clear view by a heavy tree whose branches nearly touched the ground. He had led Maylee and Smith directly in front of that spot the other night on their way to the Garden. They must have been an easy target to follow, walking right along the street, and never bothering to look behind them. *That was before we knew we were a target. We won't be making the same mistake tonight,* Rafi promised himself.

The driver sat motionless for a long time. Rafi couldn't make out his face in the dark, but he imagined him lazily watching the block. The driver moved suddenly and lifted his hand to his ear, obviously taking a phone call. After a brief conversation, he started the engine and pulled off. The plan was to follow their pursuer after all, so Rafi snatched his scooter and took off in the direction the sedan had started.

To Rafi's good fortune, a traffic light forced the driver to stop, giving him time to catch up. He followed the car for a couple miles, somewhat surprised when the driver turned towards the entrance to the Shrine of the Book museum.

"No!" he exclaimed to no one but himself. "Keep Abraham safe, Allah!" he whispered into the thin air. Disgust filled his mouth and he felt like he had swallowed gravel. The man who stepped from the car glanced nervously over his shoulder. It was just as they suspected. Amjad!

Rafi rushed back, dropped the scooter, and scaled the tree overlooking the wall separating his house from Mr. Arnold's. He began throwing rocks at Maylee and Smith's window, attempting to wake them. Breathless from excitement, Rafi struggled to express himself in his second language. Maylee placed a calming hand on his back, and she and Smith waited for him to recover. When he finally spoke, his face showed the fear that had tied knots in his intestines and caused his hands to shake. Adrenaline was coursing through his body from worry and anger.

"It's Amjad!" he gasped. "Amjad was outside guarding the street in a car, got a phone call and zoomed away. I followed him right to the Shrine of the Book!"

Smith immediately thought of the Rabbi. "Amjad was the one who drove us to drop off the scroll..."

"Did he go in with you guys?" Maylee asked.

"I don't think so," Smith stuttered. "He may have gone in while we were with Abraham, but he was still waiting for us in the car when we came out. He would have had no idea how long we were going to be inside; it would have been too risky."

"Did he know what it was you were taking so urgently to the Rabbi?" Rafi asked, leaning in intently to hear Smith's answer.

"I just don't know," Smith responded, racking his memory. "I don't think we mentioned anything specific about it, but I can't be sure."

"Maybe he doesn't know what the package contained, *insha'Allah*,"Rafi said. If Allah wills. "But he is at the museum now, and someone called him to get him there. " Rafi peered at his friends through the darkness. Slowly, reality struck them all. "He isn't working alone."

Silence reigned for a moment. Smith was the first to break it. "We have to tell Uncle Arnold!" he exclaimed. "Abraham could be in great danger, and so could the scroll."

"If we tell Uncle Arnold, our plan is doomed. He will never let us back to the Garden tonight," countered Maylee. Rafi looked torn. Whose side to take?

"It is one thing to do the wrong thing, but it is just cowardly to do the wrong thing and then lie about it," Smith announced, echoing what his uncle had told him. "I'm going to tell him! At least one man's life could depend upon it. Are you guys with me?" he asked, his tone flatly serious. Maylee and Rafi gravely nodded their agreement.

Maylee commented, "Maybe, just maybe, he will let us take him to the Garden with us."

Rafi waited anxiously in the tree as Maylee and Smith entered the little house and went to seek out their uncle. A couple of minutes later, Maylee popped her head out of the window. "He's not here" she announced, bewildered. Uncle Arnold had either never returned from work or had disappeared into the night!

TWENTY-FOUR

Betrayed

Rafi, Maylee, and Smith looked at each other, unsure what to do. Uncle Arnold, their confident, was gone. Smith glanced at his watch. It was almost 10:00. Time was ticking. They had to make a decision, and they had to make it now.

Rafi was the first to finally speak. "We have to get to the Garden," he said decidedly.

"At least Amjad isn't outside watching us right now, that we know for sure," Smith commented.

"Well," Maylee said, slapping her palms on her thighs as she stood up. "Let's do this thing then!"

"Okay, just a second," Smith said, as he popped back into the room through the window.

Rafi and Maylee stood in silence for a moment as Smith disappeared. Maylee folded her arms and swept her gaze around the tiny orchard, looking everywhere except in Rafi's direction. He, on the other hand, focused his eyes on Maylee. It was the first time just the two of them had been alone since the stairs in Monster Park.

Rafi stepped closer to her and gently taking her chin, forced her to look at him. He smiled at her and winked. She blushed, and looked up the tree, anxious for Smith's return.

"First kiss?" he asked.

She nodded without looking at him.

"Mine too," he replied.

She looked at him, surprise written on her face. "Really?"

He laughed. "Well, no. But the first one that really matters."

Maylee thought of the annoying girl with the perfect teeth and her eyes narrowed.

He reached out and pulled on one of the little curls that framed her face. It bounced back, making her blink. "Your eyes are so pretty," he said. "No one I have ever met looks like you."

Her pride ruffled its feathers. *Nah nah na-nah na,* she thought, mentally sticking out her tongue at the image of that girl. She looked up at him and they were slowly moving closer when Smith popped out of the window.

"Ready!" he announced.

Maylee blushed and turned around, folding her arms. "Finally!" she complained as she awkwardly walked towards the gate. *Breathe in, breathe out. Breathe in, breathe out,* she thought as she tried to drain the embarrassment that flushed her face and ears.

"Wait!" Rafi urged. "Let's not be so obvious in our route this time. Better safe than sorry." He led them through a gate at the back of his house after he scanned the narrow road. He motioned for them to follow, and this time, they stayed in the shadows and made their way to the Garden in silence.

Rafi motioned for Smith and Maylee to wait hidden behind a tree outside the garden while he scanned the perimeter near the little hole they were to enter through. He listened raptly for any voices or sounds that would give away anyone lurking nearby. All was clear.

He shuffled through the darkness and found Maylee and Smith once again. "Let's move," he whispered. Smith stumbled over a root that had gnarled itself over the earth before it plunged back down into the soft ground. Maylee glared at him even though it wasn't his fault. The moon wasn't out that night. It hid on the other side of the earth, like a child under the covers, afraid of what it might see that night in the Garden.

The three of them silently glided through the little hole and made their perch in the trees. They spread out as much as possible to cover more of the Garden. That way they would have the best chance of eavesdropping.

Tension filled them as they waited in silence. Their hearts beat fast and adrenaline surged through their bodies. Nothing happened. Slowly, they began to relax. An hour passed. Smith yawned and Maylee fidgeted in her tree. Smith was just opening his mouth to say "I don't think they're coming," when they heard it. He shut his mouth again.

In the distance, a twig snapped. Rafi hooted an owl's call as a warning to his two friends, the signal to remain silent.

Several minutes later, Jack stumbled through the hole, as carelessly as he had the first time. He picked himself up off the ground, looking as though he were a puppet on strings trying to convince the world he was a real boy. Big Dale slipped through behind him, and Maylee thought she could smell his sweat from where she hid.

A new face peeped through the hole, and was followed

by the petite body of a middle-aged woman. She had short, dark hair and a slim, but rather square torso. Her face was framed with black glasses, and thick, silver twists of metal snaked around her throat and wrists. *She doesn't fit in with the rest of them,* Maylee thought. *Never mind, I take that back,* she countered as she caught a glimpse of the woman's face. Her mouth was set in a grim line and her eyes glittered like beads under Jack's flashlight.

"Get that thing out of my face!" she ordered. Jack lowered the flashlight.

She was fearless. She strode confidently up to Big Dale who cowered before her, even though she was half his size. She pushed her glasses up her nose, crossed her arms, and waited in silence. Her little foot began to tap impatiently on the ground.

Heels, in the Garden? Smith thought as he caught a glimpse of a short red pump. Then it dawned on him. This was the same woman who hid the scroll in the caverns! He closed his eyes, trying to remember her voice and what she had said back in the caves the other day. He couldn't remember any details, just that the woman had been sarcastic and authoritative.

They waited in silence for what seemed an eternity. Jack sighed and plunked down on a tree root that served him as a bench. Big Dale shifted back and forth on his left and right legs, as the little woman glowered at him.

"Well, where is he?" she whined, her little dark eyes burning a hole through the fat man.

"How should I know?" he spit back out at her defensively. "I told him to be here with the scroll at midnight. I can't do any more than that!"

"Well, you had better do more than that, you big oaf!" she threatened. "Or I will just as happily take your head as a sacrifice and proof that someone died trying to get that scroll!"

As she said this she moved closer and pointed a stubby little finger right in his chest. The man flinched, obviously afraid that her words were more than an empty threat. He wiped his forehead several times with the back of his sleeve before he finally relaxed at the sound of someone approaching the Garden.

Maylee had to cover her mouth to hide a gasp as a familiar face poked through the hole. Uncle Arnold toppled through as someone shoved him from the other side. He landed on his face, his hands tied behind his back, his vision obscured by a scarf wrapped around his eyes. He was followed by Abraham's long beard that touched the ground as his face appeared in the hole. His eyes were also covered by a scarf, and although his hands weren't tied, the old man struggled to ease his tired, aged body through the tiny opening.

I knew it! thought Smith as the Israeli man who had said goodbye to them at the caverns followed shortly after. Back in the darkness at the Garden, he was sure it was the same man who had come along to bury poor Benjamin Flickermann.

Rafi shook his head and bit his lip angrily as the hole filled again with a familiar form. Amjad was the last to slither through. He smirked at Arnold with pure hatred flowing from his eyes.

Arnold stood with his head erect, exhausted, but not broken. Smith felt a wave of pride as he watched his uncle in the midst of this power-hungry group. *He is more man than the rest of them put together,* Smith thought as his uncle stood firmly, not cowering or trembling.

The little woman stepped forward, her greedy fingers itching with impatience. "Well," she said sarcastically, "are you going to hand it over, or did you want to stand here like the idiot that you are all night?"

Jerome's eyes thinned into slits as he glowered back at her. No one talked to him like that without paying for it. He would see to it that she got what she deserved.

Without a word, he reached for the backpack that Amjad handed to him. To the dismay of the three friends who watched the spectacle from the trees, he took out a flat, rectangular case. Ah, I'm glad to see you got it back!" the woman continued, a tinge of excitement thickening her voice. "And, it looks like someone did a little work on preserving it for me!

She took the top off the case and gently pulled the scroll out about an inch. Her breath came quickly as her eyes caressed it. She tucked it back inside the protective casing almost instantly. She motioned to the fat man and to Jack to exit the Garden. She was the last of the three to leave through the little hole, and just as she ducked in, she called out to Amjad and the other Israeli man. "You had better kill them," she recommended, referring to Abraham and Arnold. "Dead men can't talk."

Amjad was the one to reply this time. "With pleasure," he said, beaming.

TWENTY-FIVE

The Shrine of the Book

Jerome was the first to speak. Maylee and Smith couldn't make out his words, and they realized he was speaking Arabic. Amjad listened with rapt attention, and added in a couple comments here and there. After a brief conversation, they guided Abraham and Arnold towards the exit. The four disappeared onto the other side of the wall, and the sound of their steps faded away into the night.

Smith was shaking with rage. It was all he could do not to jump from the tree and charge Amjad and Jerome. A knife glittered in his hand. He was glad he had gone back for it. His mouth set in a grim line. "I've already lost a father," he said. "I'm not losing my uncle too!"

Rafi grabbed him by his shoulders and shook him. "Smith, you have to calm down," he commanded. "I need you to be able to help, and your anger is making you useless right now."

Smith clenched his jaw and breathing deeply, he nodded.

"What did they say?" Maylee asked anxiously.

"They are going to take them back to the Shrine of the Book," Rafi answered.

"We have to find a way to help," Smith commented, racking his brain for a solution. "We could report what happened tonight to the police," he suggested. "When we tell them about Benjamin's body that is buried nearby, they will have to at least look into what we say."

Rafi shook his head. "It would take too long," he replied. "We don't have much time. This is something we have to do on our own."

"Well?" Maylee urged, as she was about to jump through the hole in the wall. "What are we waiting for?"

Rafi and Smith followed behind her.

"The museum is only a couple of miles away," Rafi said. "I say we make a run for it."

Maylee and Smith agreed.

"Pace yourselves," Rafi ordered as he set off at a reasonable trot. They ran for nearly half an hour before they reached the museum, keeping to the shadows.

Maylee was in awe again at the size of the museum campus. It wasn't simply a block museum housing some artifacts, but a whole compound housing treasures of the past.

As they curved around the side of one of the buildings, she saw the Shrine of the Book rising into the night sky. It was in the shape of a great white funnel set with the big side down into a giant pool of water. The white rock shimmered in the night lights as water gently sprayed from a dozen little fountains around the perimeter of the pool, the drops rippling the surface of the water.

"Two-thirds of the building is actually underground," Rafi informed them. "This is just the tip of the iceberg."

"How do we get in?" Smith asked. There was no entrance cut out of the dome, just pure, white symmetry.

Rafi pointed to a tall black wall that rose out of the ground. "The entrance is behind that wall."

Maylee and Smith looked at him in question. The wall was quite a ways away.

"You enter and follow a tunnel to the dome," he explained. "It's meant to sort of replicate the caves in which the scrolls were originally discovered."

They circled the dome and found a deep set of stairs that sunk below ground level behind the basalt wall. They crept down, down, down into the darkness toward the entrance, tucking themselves in the shadows surrounding the metal door.

"Surely it's locked," Maylee whispered.

Rafi shrugged his shoulders and reached toward the door. "Couldn't hurt to try."

"Please, God. Oh, please, please, please," Smith whispered.

Rafi grasped the handle and pulled. Slowly and with a groan, the metal eased open. They stood rooted to the ground and peering into a long, dimly lit tunnel.

Cool air swirled around them, inviting them gently in. It really did feel like a cave. There was a flat, stale feel to the atmosphere that only comes from being underground. The feeling reminded Smith of being at the bottom of a huge cement parking garage.

They followed the snaking trail slowly toward the heart of the dome itself. The ceiling and walls of the tunnel gave way to what looked like the inside of a giant beehive. It was one great room whose walls were thick and close, arching their way upward into the tip of a funnel. Lining the walls were glass cases, housing copies of ancient scrolls.

In the center, a giant reproduction of a scroll pointed upward, like a rolling pin standing on its end. Wrapped around the belly of the scroll were several more slats of thick glass boasting ancient manuscripts in a 360-degree display.

As the three approached the steps that led up to the giant scroll, a quiet voice froze them in their steps. "I've been expecting you," he said calmly from behind them, his voice tinged with a British accent.

They turned to see an old man whose head looked like a speckled egg. He had the biggest ears they had ever seen. That combined with his graying skin reminded Smith of an elephant. His long, thin nose opened into great nostrils and sprouted gray nose hairs that twitched with every breath.

"Oh, I know what you are looking for," he continued, in a voice that was raspy and cracked with age. "Your uncle is currently occupied. But, since you're already here, why don't we have a little chat?" His suggestion was far more like a command, and since he was between them and the exit, they didn't really see how they had much of a choice.

"Allow me to applaud you," he said, clapping his hands slowly and circling around them. "A midnight revelry in the Garden of Gethsemane, a conversation with old al-Rashad, a visit to Abraham, a trip to Qumran and now back to the Garden tonight…" He paused, looking pointedly at each one of them as he punctuated the words, "Busy. Little. Bees." He chuckled, "And all under Amjad's watchful gaze."

He sighed thoughtfully and the gleam faded from his eyes. He looked back at them coldly, a man inclined to stop at nothing. "I knew you were in possession of the scroll for some time, probably before you really knew what you had in your hands," he began. "But, do let me explain from the beginning." He motioned for them to sit and make themselves comfortable.

"Six months ago, I was a different man. Normal, you might say. But on the night of January 12, I changed." His lips drooped as he spoke, as if the words weighed too much.

"An old friend was dying," he continued. "He called me to his deathbed and he whispered a secret to me, bringing up a ghost from my past. 'The Queen wears a disguise,' he told me, 'but she lives!'"

He was talking to himself now, convincing and justifying. "He wanted me to have the scroll. He trusted me; he knew I would protect her and never let her fall into the wrong hands." He chuckled to himself and scratched his neck with a long, delicate finger.

"But, leave it to Kareem. He died before he could tell me where she was hidden." He glanced up at them, explaining. "Oh, he tried! His mouth moved, but his dying breath suffocated his voice. I didn't sleep for weeks afterwards. All I can hear in my dreams is Kareem's tortured breathing. The 'Death Rattle' they call it. I will forever wonder what he was trying to tell me…"

"So," Smith said interrupting his thoughts, "how did you know where to look for it?"

"I didn't. Kareem's sons sold all of his things, sold 'em fast," he said, snapping his fingers to illustrate. "Before I could discover the disguise of the Queen, she had disappeared. I bought everything I could that had once belonged to Kareem, but I was only able to get my hands on a fraction of what he had accumulated. His revelation haunted me, and I have been searching ever since."

He paused in his story, holding up a withered hand as if trying to grasp the answer from the air. He turned watery eyes to the three friends and continued on with his story.

"Recently, very recently, I decided to embark on a different path. Chase another rabbit, you might say. Kareem had two grandsons, but one was a particularly wise and noble fellow who worked hard and was far a better man than his own father, Haroun. I thought that perhaps, Kareem would have chosen his grandson to protect the Queen, rather than let her fall into the hands of either of his own sons.

"I discovered that, out of all the wealth that Kareem had accumulated, he left only one thing to this favorite grandson in his death. This piqued my interest, as I assumed he would have left this young man something of great value. But, to my dismay, he left him a sentimental inheritance only—a worthless painting that Kareem had been terribly fond of."

At these words, Smith, Maylee, and Rafi exchanged a knowing glance. If the old man noticed it, he didn't show it, but rather kept talking.

"Kareem said that the Queen was in disguise, so I was expecting the scroll to be hidden in plain sight in a way that it would not be recognized, even by those who intimately knew her. I thought perhaps there was more to the painting. I went to this grandson and introduced myself as a friend of his grandfather. When the boy finally agreed to meet with me, I learned that he had taken the worthless painting from its frame and sold it to a street vendor for a fraction of it's worth.

"I begged him to remember any hints Kareem might have given him about the Queen, but he could give me no valuable information. All he could tell me was who he sold the painting to." He looked at them and raised one hairy eyebrow, gauging their reaction. "The man who bought it was none other than Benjamin Flickermann, God rest his soul."

Rafi breathed in sharply. The pieces of the puzzle were falling into place.

"Life was smiling at me. Or so I thought. All I had to do was buy the painting from Benjamin Flickermann and the Queen was mine. I called Benjamin that day to set up an appointment. I wanted to meet him after hours when no one else would be in the shop. He agreed to meet with me the following evening."

The old man paused for a long time before he continued. The guilt weighed heavy on his chest as if it were him and not Benjamin buried under a pile of dirt. "His wife Tamarah called me less than an hour before we were supposed to meet. Something had gone wrong. Benjamin had disappeared. I agreed to meet Tamarah at ARTIFACTS but I already knew deep within that this wasn't going to be good."

He paused, and linking his fingers together he stretched his arms upward. The sound of his popping knuckles overwhelmed the quiet room. Maylee pursed her lips. *I hope he has arthritis,* she thought because it was the worst thing she could wish on the terrible man in that moment.

He continued. "That was the night you all ended up in the Garden of Gethsemane," he said with a ghostly smile. "I didn't know who or how someone found out about what Benjamin had, but I knew his disappearance wasn't a coincidence. After I left ARTIFACTS, I did the only reasonable thing I could think of. I followed the grandson who sold him the painting."

He was staring at them, his face frozen in a disarming smile. The wheels were turning in their heads. Confusion and questions wrote themselves over Maylee and Smith's faces, but Rafi remained impassive. Then it dawned on her. *No!* she thought, edging her body away from her friend. *It couldn't be Rafi! But it could...*

"Wait, wait, wait," Smith said, holding his hands up. "I'm confused. How did following the grandson lead you to us?" he asked. "We didn't know anything about this until by chance we ended up in the Garden of Gethsemane that night."

The man smiled and explained. "That night was indeed a coincidence planned by the Almighty," he commented. "When you arrived in Israel, your uncle took great pains to see to it that you were safe. He didn't want you anywhere in Israel alone. The irony goes even deeper, you see, when you discover that your protector is none other than Kareem's beloved grandson!"

Without thinking, Maylee reached out a flattened hand and slapped Rafi hard across his cheek. "You traitor!" she hissed at him.

He looked at her confused and smarting from the sting on his cheek. "What did I do?" he asked, stunned.

"Not him," the old man corrected, wagging a gnarled finger at her. He leaned forward and whispered a name. "Amjad!"

What? Maylee thought. The hangnail-picking, invisible Mr. Cellophane was the grandson of one of the most powerful and wealthy men in Israel? "You have got to be kidding!" she croaked. She turned to look at Rafi. "Sorry," she mouthed.

"Not kidding," the old man said flatly. "I decided to follow Amjad after Benjamin disappeared. And he just happened to be following you."

"So, Amjad was in the Garden that night as well?" Smith asked.

"No, he didn't follow you all the way up the path. It was my sheer curiosity that led me to follow you. I knew Amjad wouldn't leave his position until you returned, so I decided I had nothing to lose. Your conversation wasn't very intriguing, however, and I was about to leave when I heard the steps behind me coming up the path. I ducked into the bushes, and the rest is history."

Maylee was only halfheartedly listening to Smith's question and the old man's response. She felt awful for suspecting Rafi. Her face turned red with shame every time she tried to look at him. And she was still processing the truth about Amjad. He had been in possession of the scroll all along and had no idea of its true value!

She tuned back in to the conversation. "I recognized Jerome," he was saying. "He is a tour guide at Qumran and works closely with the Shrine of the Book. *Curiouser and curiouser,* I thought. You see, Jerome is Kareem's other grandson. Amjad's cousin. I couldn't imagine why he was carrying a spade through the darkness."

What? Maylee's inner voice screamed. *The Israeli with no accent is Kareem's grandson too?*

The old man continued. "When I heard them mention the Queen, my suspicions were confirmed. I blamed myself for starting the rumors on the street by my questioning, and I felt guilty that the man lying dead on the ground was the result of my lack of tactfulness and caution. I knew at that point that Jerome knew the scroll's whereabouts, and I kept a careful eye on him, hoping to catch him off guard and remove the Queen from his grasp.

"It was I who forced his hand in the caverns. I disguised myself as a tourist and was on the same bus as you three," he wiggled his brows at them. I was listening to your conversation as I walked slowly to the restroom, and I learned that you too were on the right track about the Queen."

Smith looked down at the ground, embarrassed. He knew that part was his fault.

"Oh, I learned a lot that day," the old man said, reminiscing. "I found out who really wanted the scroll. Her name is Francine Davis. She's a professor of archeology in the United States and, get this," he paused for emphasis, "former mentor of Jerome when he studied in the States. She is also the proprietor of a renowned private artifacts collection."

So, that's how his accent is so perfect. He lived in the U.S. Maylee thought. *But how did Francine learn about the Queen?*

The old crow was still talking. "I had to stop the transfer of the Queen into her hands, so I blew my own cover and gave myself away to Jerome. He quickly led the party into the secret room between the corridors, and exited empty handed.

"That night, I followed them as they went to retrieve the scroll. I didn't have a plan, but I just couldn't let them take my precious Queen. To my excitement and their dismay, the scroll had vanished into thin air. I was overjoyed. At least the playing field was even again, for none of us knew where she had gone.

He turned his gaze directly on to Smith. "But I suspected the three of you. When Amjad brought you and your uncle here to the Shrine of the Book, Jerome and I both picked up the scent. I think Francine Davis assumed that it was Amjad who knew the secret of the painting, while really, he was still in the dark; it was you, Smith, and your uncle who had discovered the Queen within her disguise.

"Jerome had to get that scroll and he had to do it by tonight. Francine is…" he paused, searching for the appropriate word. "Convincing. Bold. Relentless. I have no doubt she threatened him into playing her little game."

"So, how did Jerome end up with the scroll in the Garden then, since we had already given it to Abraham?" Smith asked.

The old man beamed. "That's the beauty of all of this," he replied calmly. "He didn't!"

TWENTY-SIX

Some Answers

The three friends looked blankly at the old man. Clearly, he was crazy.

"No, wait a minute," Maylee countered. "We were just in the Garden of Gethsemane and saw Jerome give the Professor the manuscript."

The old man just shook his head. He felt it was safe to sit down beside them now. They weren't going anywhere. The old man smiled his patient, omniscient smile.

"Allow me to enlighten you," he said, casting his hand forward as if about to address a great crowd. "I will begin with what you already know and plump up the story with what happened, but what you did not see.

"After you left the Shrine of the Book, the Rabbi Abraham called me. He told me the truth, that the Queen had been found, and that he had a safe place for her to rest. But, he also asked a favor; he needed something very valuable to ensure the Queen's safety, something he could only get from me. It required a carefully and swiftly conducted guise.

"I guess I should interrupt myself and tell you something about my past. Abraham and I have been colleagues for over fifty years, but we haven't spoken for forty-five of them. While we have the highest regard for each other professionally, personally is quite another issue." His eyes clouded as he spoke.

A forty-five yearlong argument? Maylee thought. *Jeesh, I thought I had a problem holding grudges.*

"We are both good at what we do because we have a true love for preserving the past, regardless of our..." he paused, searching for the word. "Differences." He swept a hand over his pained face as if it could wipe his memory clean.

"When Abraham called me for a favor, I knew it was urgent. He called someone that he could trust rather than someone he liked."

"'Ask and it shall be given unto you...' Abraham asked and I willingly gave. I gave him a treasure, something I very much valued—a very old, ancient manuscript whose script had faded away over time." He paused and looked each of them sadly in the eye. "A document which was preserved," he croaked, "but whose message was never read.

"I knew what Abraham planned to do with it, and I supported his decision. It was the lesser of two evils." He paused and shook his head. "May God forgive us.

"To preserve the book of Esther, we conspired and defaced another ancient manuscript. Abraham took his quill and his ink and etched the very words of the book of Esther onto a false document! This imposter is the very one which Jerome took from the Rabbi earlier this evening, and which you saw exchanged in the Garden this night! The Queen rests peacefully untouched and untarnished."

No, no, no! Maylee shook her head and rubbed her temples. *This just doesn't make any sense! The scroll...the case...Uncle Arnold...*

"But, what about Uncle Arnold?" she asked. "And Amjad? What is he going to do to my uncle and the Rabbi?" Anger and confusion were rising in her voice. "And, why are we sitting here listening to you tell stories about the past rather than saving them?" Her voice was in a full-out roar now.

The old man folded his hands and closed his eyes lazily, unaffected by her outburst. "Sometimes, life is like a game of poker. You have to play with the cards you have been dealt. And to win," he said, leaning forward and opening his eyes which glittered as if he was actually thinking about winning golden coins, "to win, sometimes you have to pull off a good bluff!" He sat back and gave in to a chuckle which, to Smith, sounded quite more like a cackle.

At the sight of their unamused faces, he turned serious and explained. "As I mentioned before, Amjad was the only man in the family that Kareem thought had the necessary character to deserve the scroll as an inheritance. Amjad is a man who values things other than money and fame; he has morals and ethics that he places above convenience and profit.

"When Amjad was spying on you three tonight, I called him to get him here, to the museum. I told him Arnold was in danger. Amjad had to make a decision. He could stay and make sure that you didn't sneak out again," the old man paused to raise a hairy gray eyebrow at the three, "or he could go and see what he could do to protect his friend in what seemed to be a very serious situation. I think he likes Arnold better than you all," he mused, "because he hurried to the museum.

"Amjad convinced Jerome to allow him to help. 'I got us into this,' he said. 'At least let me be there to see that no one else will get hurt because of me. Like Benjamin.'

"You see, while I knew that the true scroll was safely tucked away, I still allowed Amjad to believe that the scroll was indeed transmitted in the Garden. Our little swap-and-go plan would come to light later.

"Having Amjad at the exchange in the Garden verified the authenticity of the scroll. Amjad was willing to play the role of traitor, as well as lose what he thought to be the true scroll in order to save his friend.

"When Amjad and Jerome showed up in the Garden, Francine assumed that Jerome and Amjad were working together and asked no questions, so long as she left with the scroll. They played the part of the bad guys in the Garden well, but they planned to release the Rabbi and your uncle at the first opportunity."

"So, where are they now?" Smith asked, his eyes big and round as two hard candies.

"Probably miserably wallowing over the fact that they lost their inheritance," he said his eyes gleaming. "We should probably go enlighten them. Come with me," he said slapping his hands on his bony knees and standing. The three hurriedly scrambled off the floor and scurried behind the old man. In spite of his age, he stood tall with his back straight and his head held proudly high.

They followed him quietly out of the dome and back along the underground corridor. He opened the metal doors and pulled out a key, locking them after him. He led them for several minutes, turning here and there as the old man moved purposefully through the labyrinth that was the campus of the Israel Museum. During the whole interaction, Rafi had remained mostly silent, his thoughts racing through his brain.

"What should we call you, sir?" he finally asked, breaking the silence.

The old man stopped as though stunned at the shattering of the silence. He looked down at the three and gave them a toothy grin. "Barker," he said, "Johann Barker."

He turned on his heel and paused, unlocking another door. It led into a short corridor that bluntly stopped at the end. *We must have made a wrong turn,* Smith thought, planning to retrace his steps. Instead, Johann Barker paused at the wall and looked deep into the stones as though he could see what was on the other side. He dug his fingertips into a groove in the wall and pressed forward. Silently, the wall swung forward, opening into a great big room with high ceilings and stuffed with expensive artifacts.

Smith's mouth dropped as he recognized sculptures and paintings of various painters and artists. They had passed around the pool surrounding the Shrine of the Book and had ended up in the store room below the museum.

A chair spun around at the other end of the room and suddenly they were face to face with Uncle Arnold. By his side, Abraham turned to face them as well, a beaming smile on his face. They were safe!

TWENTY-SEVEN

A Twist

Tamarah Flickermann sat at the table, staring blankly at the mountain of food in front of her. She hadn't been able to eat since Benjamin disappeared and the thought of food make her stomach reel. Her mother had finally left, granting her some peace. *Thank God!* she thought.

They found Benjamin's body. Her skin crawled every time she thought of him tossed carelessly into that grave and she scratched so hard she bled. Her once lovely hair was greasy, matted with the same dried blood she had under her fingernails. Worse, she didn't care. Not one little bit. She didn't want to bathe, didn't want to sleep, didn't want to live. Because all of this was just a shell. The real Tamarah was dead already. Her reason to live died when Benjamin's heart stopped beating.

In the center of the table stood a black and gold urn. All that remained of Benjamin. They had to burn him. Well, what was left of him. The maggots and bugs found him before Tamarah or the police could. She would never forget that moment of terror. The phone call. The trip to the coroner's. Identifying Benjamin. She ran her fingertip over the gold filigree of the vase as she thought.

The past week was all a blur. Her senses were dull. Only one thing was sharp in her memory. Her visit to the morgue.

They opened a metal drawer and pulled out what was left of her husband. The searing pain behind her eyes somehow brought her back to reality. She had fallen and hit her temple hard on the metal corner of the drawer in which he lay. She was face to face again with the man she loved, but his eyes were gone and his face was gray. She heard a deafening scream that made her injured head pound. Then, she realized it was her own.

Tamarah shuddered, leaving the horrid memory and coming back to the present. A strawberry on the table tempted her. She picked it up and ate half of it. She felt full again. She picked up the urn, and humming quietly to herself, made sure that the lid was on tight. She glided into her bedroom, and still holding Benjamin's remains, placed them into a backpack which she immediately strapped on.

"We will do this together, my love," she whispered. She glanced in the mirror but didn't recognize the woman who stared blankly at her with empty eyes. She turned, and tucking her thumbs tighter under the straps of the backpack, wandered barefoot into the night.

* * *

"Smith! Maylee!" Uncle Arnold cried, wrapping them simultaneously in a giant hug.

"We thought we weren't ever going to see you again," Smith said, his little blue eyes moist with tears.

"God saw fit to protect us all," Uncle Arnold soothed, "although at a very high cost." He cast a sorrowful glance at Abraham as he said the last part. The old man merely shrugged his bony shoulders under the giant black robe that dwarfed him.

"It was the Hassan's who made the final call," he said, redirecting the attention.

Jerome was the first to speak. "This is all I wanted," he said, spreading his arms around the room as he looked at each one of them. "All of you, safe."

He dropped his gaze to the floor and paused. When he spoke, his voice was almost a whisper. "It's all I wanted from the beginning. Things are just things, but people..." his voice cracked. The room was very quiet as they all waited for him to finish. "You can't replace people." They all knew he was talking about Benjamin Flickermann.

Amjad clapped his cousin on the back and began to speak. *What?* Maylee thought. *Is he actually going to take initiative and say something?* Instantly she felt guilty. *I don't have to hate him all the time, even if he is rude, extra annoying and nosy...*

"Hey," he was saying, "we all did the best we could." He looked gravely at all of them. "Everyone in this room contributed, everyone sacrificed. In the end, the bad guys got what they wanted, but not what was most valuable. This, my friends," he swept his arm around the room, "is what really matters at the end of the day."

Maylee inwardly applauded him.

Abraham cleared his throat. "Ladies and gentlemen, all is not lost. There is something I'd like to show you. Follow me, please."

He led them deeper into the holding area of the museum, stopping before an airtight glass case. It hissed at him as he opened it. He gently moved six glass frames, stopping at the seventh.

"Help an old man, would you?" he said to Rafi.

Rafi easily lifted the glass. Holding it in front of his body, he turned to face the group. Amjad inhaled sharply and Jerome sank to the floor.

"It can't be!" Jerome whispered.

"Things aren't always what they seem," Abraham said with a smile.

Rafi was about to pass the scroll to Amjad when something cold and hard at his temple stopped him. Out of the corner of his eye he could see the gray barrel of a gun.

Everyone froze for an instant. This couldn't be happening! They didn't know whether to laugh or run. Surely this wasn't for real!

Johann spoke in a calm voice, as if he could read their thoughts. "This is the real deal, Rafi. While I've never killed anyone before, I feel very confident that I won't have any problem doing it here tonight. The Queen is mine! Kareem wanted me to have it. I have spent my entire life looking for this and I'm not going to let it go now that I finally have it in my grasp."

Rafi looked intently at Abraham. *What should I do?* he asked with his eyes.

"Give him the scroll, Rafi," Abraham commanded.

Rafi hesitated. Johann shoved the barrel deeper into his skull, jarring Rafi's neck with the force. Slowly, Rafi passed the glass to Johann who grasped it with his left hand.

"I need you to walk me out, if you would," still keeping the gun pointed at Rafi's head. "I suggest you don't follow me if you want Rafi back alive." As they were about to exit the holding room, Johann paused. He turned, settling an intense gaze on Abraham.

"I can't let you win twice. I can't let you have both of the women we loved," he said sadly.

"It's not the same, Johann," he responded quietly. "Alice had a choice. I can see now why she chose me."

Johann spat on the ground. "The Queen is mine!" he whispered. He scurried out through the dim passage and disappeared from their sight, taking Rafi with him as a hostage.

"Is he going to hurt him?" Maylee's voice was wobbly.

"I don't think so," Abraham answered. "He is blinded right now by The Queen. Nothing else matters. I think he will let Rafi go after he makes his escape."

Amjad picked at his fingernails. It had been a long night of ups and downs. Scroll, no scroll; scroll, no scroll. He sighed. He had been better off before he even knew the scroll existed.

Uncle Arnold paced back and forth, back and forth across the length of the room. *Why didn't I see this coming? Stupid, stupid, stupid!*

Maylee and Smith sat close together on the floor, suddenly unaware of all the riches around them. Only one thing mattered right now. "Rafi is gonna be okay," Smith whispered. Maylee nodded her head. She really needed to believe that.

It seemed like an eternity before they heard hesitant footsteps approaching. Maylee leapt off the ground and bolted to the passageway before anyone could stop her. She ran right into Rafi's arms and swallowed him up in a huge hug. "I was so worried! If anything had happened to you, I..."

"Shh," he comforted her. "I'm here, I'm okay." She released him so that her uncle and the Rabbi could embrace him as well.

"Let's go home," Uncle Arnold offered. No one argued.

TWENTY-EIGHT

Sweet Revenge

Johann walked slowly to his car, placed the scroll in the seat next to him, and buckled his seat belt. *No rush,* he thought. *Those cowards aren't coming after me. They are too worried about their precious friends to fight for something really valuable.*

He went the speed limit all the way home. He knew he was going to have to leave the country. *Those idiots will probably call the police rather than deal with this themselves.* The thought made him angry. Why couldn't they just let him be happy, alone with his Queen?

He entered his house and began loading up the bags he had already packed. He was prepared for this. His ticket to Cairo lay waiting for him on his desk. He smirked. Hadn't Jesus' family fled to Egypt when the authorities were pursuing them? *What would Jesus do?* He chuckled to himself. He was so very clever.

The Queen's disguise was ready. He broke her out of the glass she was housed in, and slipped her inside another blanket of a painting. It had worked so well for Kareem, why not for him as well? Carefully, he sealed the painting and smiled, pleased with the finished product.

He slipped out to the car and was about to open the door when suddenly, a very bright light seared his brain. He fell to the ground and his knees hit hard on the cold cement. What was happening?

He was having a hard time breathing. His mouth filled with a warm liquid that tasted sharply of metal. He spat it out on the ground. It was dark and sticky. He was getting his vision back. Painfully, he rolled over on his back and stared up at the starlit sky.

The silhouette of a woman stood over him, a small revolver in her hand. His own revolver, Johann faintly realized. The one he kept in his desk.

"Your fault," Tamarah Flickermann whispered. She looked him squarely in the face and shot him again. He heard his ribs crack as the bullet forced its way into his chest. When she was sure he was dying, she tossed the gun on the ground with her gloved hand, away from his reach. She turned, and tucking her thumbs tightly under the backpack she wore, padded softly along the cobblestones, her bare feet noiseless in the night.

Johann could feel the life oozing out of him. He stretched his arm behind him, his fingers reading the ground like braille. The Queen lay just out of his reach. He struggled to grasp the scroll until the very end. And then, Johann Barker learned what it felt like to die alone.

* * *

The next morning, Mrs. Adler stepped outside to water her flowers. She dropped the hose and let out a terrified scream before she ran inside and called the police.

"My neighbor, Johann Barker, is lying dead in a puddle of blood next to my aloe plants," she told them.

Within half an hour, there were officers and emergency personnel crawling all over the lawn. Mrs. Adler was furious.

A man named Youseff Arafat was in charge. He yawned, and wished he were back in his office. The thrill of a new crime scene had worn off for him years ago.

Well, it's definitely too late for an ambulance, Youseff thought, eying the medical vehicle he had arrived in. "Bring the body bag, guys. Crime scene unit is done with him now."

"What should we do with all this stuff?" an intern asked him, pointing to the loaded car.

Youseff tossed him a roll of plastic bags. "Go ahead and bag it, Layth," he said. "Next of kin will eventually get to go through it."

Layth raised his hand to his forehead in salute. "You got it."

Layth placed the keys, wallet, and a hairbrush into a separate bag. Personal belongings and an easy DNA sample, should they need it.

Really? he thought, looking down at the body they were just covering. *Did you really think you needed a hairbrush, dude?* He shook his head. The old man was basically bald.

He piled the bags he filled behind the car. Someone would pick them up, he was told.

He circled the car once more and saw something peeking out by the tire. He stooped down to pull it out. It was a painting of a fairy. Cheap, but cute.

He wouldn't have thought twice about the painting, but his seven-year-old daughter was in that fairy-and-princesses phase. He glanced around. The ambulance was gone. The crime scene unit was loading up their vehicle. Quickly, he stashed the painting in one of the plastic bags and tossed it in his own truck.

"Anything else, boss?" he asked Youseff.

Youseff shook his head. "You're good to go."

Layth hopped in his vehicle, pausing to wave at the rest of the crew before he headed home. His daughter Maysaa was going to love this!

ACKNOWLEDGMENTS

Because of my nephew Joseph, to whom this book is dedicated, I was inspired to read various young adult books, and realized just how much fun it can be. I'd like to say a special thank-you to my nephews and nieces, who keep me young and who sometimes inspire teenage-like behavior in me.

To my dear mom, who listened to me talk about these characters as if they were family and who tirelessly read every version of the manuscript (and there were many), I cannot give enough of my deepest gratitude. Although you never had the chance to see the published version, you are present in every page. I love you forever.

Erika Vargas, thank you for sitting me down regularly and encouraging me to write; in spite of my desires to do something easier, you have seen my potential and challenged me to achieve it. Press on, soul sister.

To my brother, Matt, who printed off the first draft of my manuscript for review and who came up with the series name, Quest for the Queen—thank you for being an inspiration, a role-model, and my dear friend.

Lori, thank you for teaching me to *really* read—to fall into a story, to slip between the pages, to unlock the story tied up in the words. Thank you for encouraging me to finish this book, and thank you for your patience along the way.

Much love to you all.